Will You Marry Me?

Popping the Question With Romance and Style

JASON R. RICH

New Page Books
a division of the Career Press, Inc.
Franklin Lakes, NJ

WILL YOU MARRY ME?
EDITED AND TYPESET BY CLAYTON W. LEADBETTER
Cover design by Lu Rossman/Digi Dog Design
Printed in the U.S.A. by Book-mart Press

To order this title, please call toll-free 1-800-CAREER-1 (NJ and Canada: 201-848-0310) to order using VISA or MasterCard, or for further information on books from Career Press.

The Career Press, Inc., 3 Tice Road, PO Box 687,
Franklin Lakes, NJ 07417
www.careerpress.com
www.newpagebooks.com

Library of Congress Cataloging-in-Publication Data

Rich, Jason.
    Will you marry me? : popping the question with romance and style / by
Jason R. Rich.
        p. cm.
    Includes index.
    ISBN 1-56414-717-7 (pbk.)
        1. Courtship. 2. Commitment (Psychology) 3. Marriage proposals.
4. Betrothal. I. Title.

HQ801.A5R53 2004
306.73'4—dc21   2003059959

Acknowledgments

or helping to make my life so special, I'd like to thank the Bendremer family (Ellen, Sandy, and Emily), Ferras, Mark, and my family. These are the people who provide me with love, support, and guidance each and every day.

In terms of this book, my sincere gratitude goes out to the folks at Harry Winston, BlueNile.com (especially John Baird and Brian Watkins), plus everyone at Korbel Champagne Cellars and Edelman Worldwide (especially to Julie Schweigert, Susu Block, Devin Collins, and Caroline Dettman). Thanks also to all of the people and organizations that provided me with the proposal ideas used throughout this book.

At The Career Press/New Page Books, many thanks to Ron Fry and Mike Lewis for their ongoing support and for inviting me to work on this project. Thanks also to everyone else at New Page Books who helped make this book a reality, including Stacey Farkas, Clayton Leadbetter, Kirsten Beucler, and Anne Brooks.

Finally, thanks to you, the reader, who has turned to this book for ideas, advice, and support as you plan how you'll pop the question and ultimately get engaged.

Contents

Goodbye

Bachelorbood

ill You Marry Me? is all about how you can propose marriage to your girlfriend—or boyfriend—in the most memorable way possible, based upon your relationship, personalities, and dreams. Whether this will be your first marriage or your fifth, this book will help you make the proposal process more exciting and romantic. As you're about to discover, there are countless ways to propose that can incorporate tradition, humor, religious or spiritual beliefs, and romance. How you ultimately "pop the question" should relate directly to the relationship you have with your significant other. This book is chock full of ideas to help you create the most memorable and exciting marriage proposal possible.

While the context in which this book was written focuses on the typical guy proposing to his girlfriend, the same information holds true for women looking to propose to their boyfriends, as well as to gay or lesbian couples looking to make a more formal commitment to each other. In other words, if you're looking to propose to your "significant other," this book will help you do it in a fun, innovative, and romantic way.

Most women have dreamed of their storybook-like marriage proposal and wedding since they were little girls. It's common for young girls to create and act out their dream proposal and wedding over and over again, using their dolls. If you're a guy proposing to your girlfriend, now that you're both adults, it's your job to transform your girlfriend's childhood fantasy into a reality as you prepare to give up your bachelorhood and dedicate yourself to the person you love.

However, according to research conducted by Korbel Champagne Cellars, six out of 10 Americans do not think that men should always be the ones to propose. Furthermore, eight out of 10 guys would definitely accept a marriage proposal from their girlfriend. The tradition of the guy always proposing to the girl is definitely changing. Nearly 70 percent of all Americans now believe it's socially acceptable for women to propose marriage to men. So, if you're sick of waiting for your boyfriend to ask for your hand in marriage, consider taking control of the situation and proposing to him.

Are you nervous? Well, you should be! Once you pop the question and become engaged, your life as you know it will change forever—hopefully for the better! Leading up to your wedding, however, you need to find the perfect engagement ring; decide how and when you want to propose; actually make the proposal; then, as a newly engaged couple, plan your wedding; and, ultimately, get married. You're in for exciting and unforgettable times ahead!

This book is all about the marriage proposal process. Once you've decided that you've met the perfect spouse and you know you want to get engaged, this book walks you through the process of finding and buying the perfect diamond engagement ring. As you'll soon discover, this can be a confusing, time-consuming, and frustrating experience if you're not totally prepared. *Will You Marry Me?* also offers dozens of ideas to help you pop the question in the most exciting, fun, and memorable way possible, whether you want to propose in a traditional manner or turn it into an extravagant event.

Finally, this book will help you compile a preproposal checklist to ensure that you're able to flawlessly enact the proposal you envision, then deal with all of the details relating to your proposal idea (whether or not it's accepted). Once you're engaged, the final chapter of this book will help you prepare for the many changes that will quickly occur in your life. At this point, you'll probably want to formally announce your engagement to friends, family, and coworkers; plan an engagement party; and start making plans for your wedding.

As you proceed, you must prepare to leave your single life behind, have your life as you know it turned upside down, tear up your little black book, and dedicate your life to the one you love—your future spouse. You're about to embark on an exciting, challenging, and fun part of your life. It's a time you'll remember, hopefully fondly, for many years to come!

Your Life Is About to Change Dramatically

Whether you realize it or not, the moment you seriously start contemplating getting engaged, your life is going to change dramatically. At the very least, you will no longer be able to date other people, because you'll be in a serious, monogamous, and committed relationship.

Once you decide you're ready to get engaged and eventually be married, you'll automatically be taking on a series of huge responsibilities, starting with finding and buying the perfect engagement ring (see Chapter 1), then deciding how and when you'll actually propose. After the proposal, you'll officially be engaged, which means you'll need to begin making wedding plans—and prepare to start your new life together as husband and wife.

From the moment you pop the question, events in your life will happen quickly and may seem like they're spinning out of control. This is totally normal, albeit somewhat overwhelming.

If you've truly found your soul mate, you should be very happy, proud, and excited! Being in love is a wonderful feeling. Having the opportunity to share the rest of your life with someone whom you love, cherish, trust, and respect is an incredible thing, so consider yourself extremely lucky! From the moment you get engaged, you'll potentially never be alone again. You will have a partner with whom you can confront every one of life's challenges and obstacles, but at the same time, enjoy life.

Getting engaged and ultimately married is a major deal in your life. Treat it as such, but remember to enjoy every moment that goes into the planning of your proposal, wedding, and your future lives together. The rest of this book assumes you've already met the person of your dreams and plan to pop the question in the not-so-distant future. Thus, it will walk you through every major step in the process, starting with finding and buying the perfect diamond engagement ring—which has become a tradition when it comes to getting engaged.

Chapter 1

Finding and Buying the Perfect Engagement Ring

It's been said that "diamonds are a girl's best friend." Any guy who has presented his girlfriend will a diamond engagement ring, and has seen the look in her eyes and the expression on her face as this symbol of eternal love is presented during a proposal, will surely agree with this statement. When a woman gets engaged, aside from hopefully finding the man of her dreams, the pride she typically feels when showing off her engagement ring to friends, coworkers, relatives (and everyone else she meets) is unparalleled. After all, by showing off her engagement ring, she's able to brag that she's about to marry the person she feels is the greatest guy in the world, her soul mate and true love.

While it's certainly not mandatory that a guy present a diamond engagement ring to his girlfriend upon proposing, this practice has become a tradition. These days, upwards of 78 percent of all brides receive a diamond ring at the time of their engagements.

Finding and buying the perfect engagement ring is not an experience you will soon forget. This chapter is all about helping you obtain the knowledge you need to make intelligent decisions as you embark on your quest to find an engagement ring for your girlfriend that fits within your budget, yet symbolizes all of the powerful feelings of love and affection you feel for her.

Once Upon a Time: A Bit of History

Since the 14th century, when couples decide to get married, a symbol of their love and commitment to each other has been the diamond engagement ring. It's believed that in 1477, the tradition began with Archduke Maximillian of Australia proposing to Mary of Burgundy. At the time, diamonds were believed to be magical charms that could enhance the love a husband had for his wife.

According to ADiamondIsForever.com, it wasn't until the 1870s, when the diamond mines were discovered in Africa, that diamonds became more accessible to everyday people, and the tradition of presenting a diamond engagement ring was born. The tradition for the woman to wear her engagement ring on the fourth finger of her left hand, however, dates back to ancient Egypt. It was believed that the *vena amoris* (the vein of love) ran from that finger straight to the heart.

While superstitions and the belief in magic may be outdated, the presentation of a diamond engagement ring to a woman continues to be a popular part of the marriage proposal process. Perhaps it's because a diamond is one of the hardest, most beautiful, and most valuable substances on Earth that it has become the symbol of love a man presents to a woman when he proposes marriage.

It takes the Earth millions of years to create a diamond, but it also takes the work of a skilled craftsman or diamond cutter to cut that diamond and create a stunning piece of jewelry with it. It's this piece of jewelry that can be a lasting symbol of your love and commitment as you get engaged to be married. It's also a piece of jewelry that will be worn proudly, hopefully for the rest of your future wife's life.

The Perfect Engagement Ring

For the guy, buying the perfect engagement ring can be a tremendous challenge. An independent survey of more than 1,200 men and women, conducted on behalf of BlueNile.com (a company to which you'll be introduced later in this chapter), revealed that 75 percent of men do not feel knowledgeable about jewelry. As a result, purchasing the perfect engagement ring raises the stakes considerably. After all, what exactly is the "perfect" ring? If you follow the common belief that the ring you choose is a direct representation of the love you have for the woman to whom you're proposing, then you might believe that the perfect ring would contain at least a 3- to 5-carat diamond, with a one-of-a-kind, custom designed platinum setting. The problem is, most people don't have $175,000 to $350,000 (or more) to spend on an engagement ring.

How much are you going to spend? That's totally up to you. Some people cap their engagement ring budget at two or three months' salary, however, there are no rules. Because virtually all jewelers offer financing options, you can often combine your savings, credit cards, and the financing plans offered by the jeweler to purchase the ring you (and your soon-to-be fiancée) truly desire. The trick, however, is to spend an amount that you're comfortable with, based on the ring you select. Ultimately, you'll want to set a realistic budget for yourself, then find a ring that you think will take your girlfriend's breath away and symbolize your feelings of love for her.

Purchasing a diamond engagement ring (or any piece of jewelry, for that matter) is a combination of personal taste, preference, and science. While there is no formula to follow for purchasing the perfect engagement ring, there are quantifiable characteristics that can help you find the diamond that best fits your need and budget. This chapter explains some of the technical knowledge you'll need to make an educated buying decision, plus strategies for determining what your girlfriend really wants her ring to be like.

Remember, a diamond engagement ring is a *symbol* of your love and commitment, not a *measure* of it. Thus, you'll want to select a ring that's within your budget, but that's stunning and that the woman to whom you're proposing will cherish forever. What? You think that's a lot of pressure to put on a guy about to make a major purchase? Consider this: Modernbride.com conducted a poll in which "We asked brides-to-be: How many times a day do you admire your engagement ring?" The results were: 1 to 10 times—41.4 percent, 11 to 25 times—17.4 percent, and "almost constantly"—41.2 percent.

To find the perfect engagement ring, prepare to invest not just your money, but your time and energy. First, however, obtain some basic knowledge about diamonds and precious metals, then apply that knowledge, combined with your personal tastes and what you know of your girlfriend's tastes, to make the right purchase decision.

As you proceed in making this significant purchase, remember that you're acquiring a work of art, a rare and valuable gem—plus a symbol of your love. This isn't at all like making a nonemotional financial investment. It is possible, however, to understand what you're buying and use that information to your advantage.

What You Need to Know Before You Start Ring Shopping

If you're buying a diamond engagement ring, the most important aspect of that purchase is the actual diamond. The stone you choose will play a major role in determining the price, value, and overall quality of the ring. The price you ultimately pay for the diamond, however, will be based on multiple criteria.

All diamonds are priced based upon four quantifiable characteristics—*cut*, *clarity*, *carat*, and *color*. These are the four Cs you'll need to understand when selecting, pricing, and ultimately purchasing your diamond. Once you select the diamond, the next step is choosing the perfect gold, white gold, or platinum setting for that diamond.

The following sections will help you better understand how the four Cs relate to diamonds, as well as provide you with other valuable knowledge about precious metals when purchasing the perfect engagement ring.

Finally, don't be afraid to shop around, compare prices and quality, visit multiple jewelers, and ask plenty of questions throughout the entire process. In the end, you want to be comfortable, confident, and totally happy with your purchase. You should equate selecting and purchasing an engagement ring to buying a new home or car, as opposed to a new pair of shoes. Put some time, thought, and research into your decision.

Choosing Your Diamond: Understanding the Four Cs

When you start working with one or more jewelers and visiting jewelry stores (or online jewelry retailers) in search of the perfect diamond engagement ring, you're going to hear a lot about cut, clarity, carat, and color.

Yes, it's important to understand how each of these criterium is used to evaluate, grade, and price a diamond. However, don't just attempt to memorize and understand this information from a theoretical standpoint. As you deal with jewelers, ask to see examples of actual diamonds and have the jeweler show you exactly how cut, clarity, carat, and color impact each diamond's beauty and cost. In other words, look at the diamonds themselves and try to understand their differences.

To help you understand how diamonds are graded, point your Web browser to *www.ags.org/public/howtobuy/chart.htm*. Print out the chart provided by The American Gem Society and take it with you to the jewelers when you actually look at diamonds.

The Diamond's Cut

In terms of beauty, the *cut* of a diamond is the single-most important characteristic. It is the quality of cut that has the greatest impact on brilliance and fire. Brilliance allows the diamond to shimmer, shine, and reflect the light. A well-cut diamond creates the beautiful flashes of red, green, blue, violet, and yellow prismatic colors that we see as fire. In this case, the term *cut* refers directly to the angles and proportions of the diamond itself. This should not be confused with the diamond's shape.

You'll soon discover, when you begin shopping for diamonds, that the most popular diamond shapes for an engagement ring (listed in alphabetical order) include:

- Baguette (Straight or Tapered).
- Emerald.
- Heart.
- Marquis.
- Oval.
- Pear.
- Princess.
- Radiant.
- Round.
- Square.
- Triangle.
- Trillion.

The following photos show diamonds cut in some of these popular shapes. As you can see, the shape of the diamond will have a dramatic impact on the overall appearance of the engagement ring.

The Blue Nile Signature Collection Princess Diamond is custom made exclusively for Blue Nile. It is the world's first and only ideal cut princess diamond. The exacting dimensions of each Signature Collection Diamond places it among the top one percent of diamonds in the world. Copyright Blue Nile, Inc.

From Blue Nile, this is a round-cut diamond engagement ring in a classic four-prong setting with round channel-set diamonds throughout. Copyright Blue Nile, Inc.

*An emerald-shaped diamond.
Copyright Blue Nile, Inc.*

*A heart-shaped diamond.
Copyright Blue Nile, Inc.*

*A marquis-shaped diamond.
Copyright Blue Nile, Inc.*

An oval-shaped diamond.
Copyright Blue Nile, Inc.

A pear-shaped diamond.
Copyright Blue Nile, Inc.

A princess-shaped diamond.
Copyright Blue Nile, Inc.

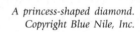

A radiant-shaped diamond.
Copyright Blue Nile, Inc.

A round-shaped diamond.
Copyright Blue Nile, Inc.

Each diamond is cut according to specific mathematical formulas. Diamonds.com reports, "Diamonds are usually cut with 58 facets, or separate flat surfaces. These facets follow a mathematical formula and are placed at precise angles in relation to each other. This relationship is designed to maximize the amount of light reflected through the diamond and to increase its beauty." (A diamond's *facets* are the small, flat, polished planes designed to reflect light.) The formula used to cut each shape of diamond is different.

While the Earth creates the diamond over millions of years, the cut and shape is determined by man. To properly cut a diamond to give it the most beauty and value requires a tremendous level of skill, because every angle and plane must be accurately calculated. The quality of a diamond's cut is graded. An *ideal cut* is considered the best. Working down the scale, a diamond's cut can be graded as *excellent, very good, good, fair,* or *poor.*

According to The American Gem Society:

> *An ideal cut refers to a diamond that has been shaped to its optimum proportions for maximum brilliance. To realize an ideal cut, the cutter must adhere to a series of exacting tolerances. And to achieve this, much of the rough diamond may need to be cut away. For these reasons, ideal cut is the exception rather than the rule. In fact, less than one percent of all diamonds cut are cut to ideal proportions for maximum brilliance.*

To properly evaluate a stone's cut, seek out the advice and assistance of a skilled and experienced gemologist, who has been trained to evaluate a diamond's cut using what The American Gem Society refers to as, "either a precise millimeter gauge which measures width, depth, crown height and pavilion depth or by using a projection image known as a proportionscope." With recent technological advancements, there are software programs with dedicated hardware that will mathematically measure a diamond's specific parameters. It is important to review the diamond's GIA or AGS certification (to be discussed shortly) and not simply rely on the word of a gemologist, jeweler, or jewelry salesperson who may not have the equipment to report this information accurately.

The cut of a diamond is a major factor in determining its value. An ideal cut diamond offers the most brilliance and tends to be the most costly. If a diamond is cut poorly, it will appear dull and have less value.

The Diamond's Clarity

Most diamonds contain natural imperfections that detract from their value and clarity. In many cases, when you're dealing with quality diamonds, these imperfections or inclusions are extremely tiny and are found within the diamond itself. If there is an inconspicuous irregularity on the diamond's surface, it's called a *blemish*. To properly identify imperfections/inclusions and blemishes, an expert will view the diamond under 10x magnification. The frequency, size, color, type, and location of the inclusions and blemishes are used to determine a diamond's *clarity*.

Typically, inclusions and blemishes are not visible to the naked eye, thus, while the visual beauty of the diamond may not be affected, the presence of any minor imperfections will detract from its rarity and value. When you're shopping for a diamond, you'll probably want one with the highest clarity you can afford. The experts at Blue Nile recommend selecting an "eye-clean" diamond:

This is one that has no inclusions visible to the unaided eye. An excellent value, diamonds of this clarity are much less expensive than FL-grade [flawless] diamonds and typically do not contain visible inclusions that detract from the beauty of the diamond. If you'd rather not compromise on clarity, yet are budget conscious, choose a diamond with a good cut and G or H color. [More detailed information about color will be discussed in an upcoming section.]

As you look at diamonds, study them with your naked eye, but also ask to view them under a gem binocular microscope at 10x magnification. While you do this, have the jeweler explain what you're looking at and point out the inclusions and blemishes of each particular diamond you look at.

The Gemological Institute of America (GIA) implemented a color and clarity grading system that is universally used today. The American Gem Society (AGS) has an exclusive diamond grading system for rating cut, color, and clarity, but also provides the GIA equivalent for comparison. When shopping for your diamond, make sure you see the actual GIA and/or AGS report. Don't settle for a report from another organization with a similar name that is not internationally recognized and accepted.

According to Diamonds.com, "A diamond's clarity is graded using a very precise and complex method of evaluating the size, location and visibility of inclusions." A "flawless" diamond, for example, shows absolutely no inclusions or blemishes under 10x magnification. These are among the rarest and most valuable diamonds.

An "Internally Flawless" diamond is one that contains no internal inclusions (under 10x magnification), but has some minor external blemishes. For a more detailed description of how a diamond's clarity is rated, see the following chart.

GIA and AGS Diamond Clarity Ratings		
GIA Rating	**AGS Rating**	**Explanation**
Flawless (FL)	0	The diamond contains no inclusions or blemishes under 10x magnification.
WS1 or WS2	1 or 2	The diamond contains very slight inclusions that are difficult to spot under 10x magnification—even by experienced graders.
VS1 or VS2	3 or 4	Diamonds that receive this clarity rating contain very slight inclusions, such as crystals, clouds, or feathers (types of inclusions) when viewed under 10x magnification.
SI1 or SI2	5 or 6	A diamond rated with this clarity contains inclusions that are obvious when viewed under magnification. According to Diamonds.com, "A laboratory-certified clarity rating of SI2 represents the point at which inclusions are technically not apparent to the average naked eye."
I1, I2, or I3	7, 8, 9, or 10	Diamonds that receive one of these clarity ratings contain larger inclusions that are obvious and that impact the diamond's transparency and brilliance. These inclusions can be seen with the naked eye, thus making diamonds with these clarity ratings the least valuable and the most common.

The Diamond's Carat

The common misconception is that a diamond's *carat* is related to its physical size. More accurately, however, a diamond's carat is a measurement of its weight. One carat is equal to 200 milligrams (0.2 grams or 1/142 of an ounce). In terms of measuring the diamond, a 1-carat (1.00 ct) diamond is divided into 100 *points*, each worth 1/100th of a carat. Thus, a diamond that weighs 100 milligrams might be referred to as a 50-point diamond or a 1/2-carat diamond (0.50 ct).

Another misconception about diamonds is that a one-carat diamond would cost exactly twice the price of a half-carat diamond, for example, assuming their cut, color, and clarity are otherwise identical. This is not the case, however. Larger diamonds are rarer, thus disproportionately more valuable.

A one-carat diamond can cost several times that of a half-carat diamond. A 0.50 carat diamond with D color, that's internally flawless and rated with an ideal cut might cost around $4,000. An otherwise identical diamond that's 1.50 carats, however, could easily cost $30,000.

The Diamond's Color

When it comes to diamonds, the most expensive and rare diamonds are the colorless ones. These diamonds are rated D. The rating system for *color* begins at D (colorless) and continues alphabetically through Z. Diamonds that have color may contain trace elements (measured in parts per million), causing them to appear light yellow, brownish, grayish, or cloudy.

Accurately grading a diamond's color requires a laboratory with very precise equipment. When you're buying a diamond, always look for a certification from an independent laboratory, such as the GIA or AGS, for an accurate and reliable color rating for the stone you're looking at.

For a diamond engagement ring, a diamond with a color grade of J or better is usually best and falls in a reasonable price range (but price also depends heavily on other factors, such as carat, cut, and clarity). Diamonds with a color grade of J or better will typically appear colorless to the naked eye when mounted (even if they aren't truly colorless.) Stones with a K through V color grade will be visibly yellowish or discolored to the naked eye, even when mounted. Stones with X, Y, or Z grades have significant color and are generally very attractive, but are very rare and difficult to find. It's sometimes possible to camouflage the slightly yellowish tint of a lower color-graded diamond by mounting it in yellow gold (as opposed to white gold or platinum).

While the cost of a D-rated diamond will be higher than an E- or F-rated diamond (when focusing on color), to the naked eye, the color difference can generally only be seen by a diamond expert. For this reason, always look at the diamond with your own eyes and choose the one you find aesthetically pleasing. Once you know the diamond color range you can afford, ask to see similar diamonds (in terms of cut, clarity, and carat) but with slightly different color grades. You might like an F-rated diamond, for example, because it will look better than a particular D- or E-rated diamond in the type of mounting you've selected.

Keep in mind, however, that while trace elements may discolor a diamond (keeping it from being graded as colorless), some of the most rare and expensive diamonds in the world come in "fancy colors"—shades of pink, blue, green, amber, and red. Fancy colored diamonds follow their own color grading system.

The Fifth and Sixth Cs: Confidence and Cost

Ultimately, you'll want to develop a strong and trusting relationship with a reputable jeweler when you purchase the engagement ring. When it comes to working with any type of specialist, the best way to find an expert is from a personal referral or recommendation. Talk to friends or family members who have purchased an engagement ring or other fine jewelry in the past, and ask for the name of the jeweler with whom he or she conducted business. Another good source to find unbiased recommendations is the Internet.

The various resources listed at the end of this chapter can also be used to find a reputable jeweler. Once you find a jeweler you believe you can trust and you're comfortable working with, rely on their expertise and training to help you choose the ideal ring. Your purchase must be made with confidence. You should be comfortable that what you're spending is based upon your budget and that you're actually getting the best value for your money, in terms of quality.

While the price of a comparable diamond should be consistent from jeweler to jeweler, the ultimate cost of the ring (complete with diamond and setting) is somewhat subjective. The metal chosen for the band, the addition of side stones, and any customization done to the ring will influence the price. This being the case, similar rings can have vastly different prices.

What You Need to Know About Ring Settings

As you're selecting your diamond, begin to consider the setting style and how you'd like your stone to be set. The *setting* or *ring mounting* refers to the actual ring band, typically made from platinum, gold, or white gold. The *setting method* or *head* refers to how the diamond is held in place within the setting. Every jeweler you visit will showcase different designs and styles to choose from. Thus, it becomes a matter of personal taste and functionality when choosing a ring.

One of the decisions you'll need to make relates to the type of metal the setting (band) will be made of. The most common selections are 18-karat yellow gold, white gold or platinum. While yellow gold is the most popular, platinum has dramatically increased in popularity in recent years, because of its brilliant sparkle and durability. White gold is the least popular of the three.

When it comes to jewelry, platinum is the strongest and purest metal. Platinum jewelry typically uses platinum that's 90 to 95 percent pure, meaning it will be strong, resistant to scratches and chips, and will not tarnish. If you prefer yellow gold, 18-karat (18k) will provide you the best combination of luster and strength. White gold is made by adding nickel to the yellow gold and then plating it with rhodium, an incredibly hard metal alloy that enhances the "white" appearance and prevents tarnish. Keep in mind, when choosing between the different metals, that platinum is stronger and more durable than gold, but gold's soft qualities makes it easier to repair, should it become damaged. The rhodium plating on white gold will wear over time. It is a good idea to have white gold replated every few years—the cost of this process is nominal.

As you'll quickly discover, there are countless setting styles. Some offer a timeless and classic look, while others offer a more modern or flashy design. A *solitaire setting* (a single diamond mounted in the center of the gold or platinum band) is the most popular setting style and usually offers a timeless look. When selecting this type of setting, you'll need to choose how the stone will be mounted. Popular options include a four-prong or six-prong mounting. As you'd expect, a six-prong head with platinum studs typically covers a bit more of the actual diamond, but it is more secure.

Some engagement ring settings offer side stones. These are diamonds or other gemstones that surround or somehow compliment the main diamond. The number of different styles and setting variations when you add side stones to the ring are virtually limitless. What you ultimately choose becomes a matter of personal taste and budget.

As you choose the engagement ring's style, think ahead. After all, you'll also be presenting your bride with a wedding ring (which is typically worn on the same finger as the engagement ring). You'll want the two rings to match (or at least coordinate well together). Also, do you want the engagement ring to match other jewelry your soon-to-be fiancée already owns (or will own in the future), such as diamond earrings, necklaces, and bracelets?

Consider the lifestyle of the wearer. Is your girlfriend extremely active? Would it be better to purchase a more durable ring so she doesn't have to keep taking it off her finger when she engages in certain activities?

As you consider your ring's style and a preferred method of setting your stone, consider the many different diamond shapes. The same setting will look totally different with a round diamond as opposed to a pear shaped or heart shaped diamond, for example. Likewise, a round diamond in a platinum setting will look dramatically different than in a yellow gold setting. Mix and match diamond shapes and settings until you discover what you believe is the perfect engagement ring.

Following are some Websites that offer interactive custom ring design applications where you can mix and match diamonds with settings to create the perfect virtual engagement ring on your computer screen.

- ❧ BlueNile.com (800-242-2728, *www.bluenile. com*)—This jeweler has successfully sold more than 35,000 diamond engagement rings via the Internet. The company's Website offers an abundance of useful information about buying an engagement ring, as well as an easy-to-use application that allows you to create a custom engagement ring on your computer screen, then price and purchase your creation. Point your web browser to *www.bluenile.com/engagement_choose_ diamond.asp*.

- ❧ A Diamond Is Forever (*www.adiamondisforever. com*)—This Website also offers a free feature that allows you to create your own customized diamond engagement ring on your computer screen. The process begins once you complete a short questionnaire about your personal situation. Next, you'll be asked to choose a diamond cut (shape), type of metal for the setting, and whether you want to add side stones. You'll then see a full-color virtual depiction of your ring on the screen, which can ultimately be saved, printed, or e-mailed. A Diamond Is Forever is an information resource, not an online retailer. Thus, you cannot purchase the diamond ring you create online. The site was created to help people learn about the diamond buying process.

Size Matters: The Right Ring Size

Just like clothing and shoes, a ring must be properly sized to fit on someone's finger. However, accurately determining your girlfriend's ring size can be one of the biggest challenges in purchasing the ring. You need not let this consideration perplex you, as any reputable jeweler will resize the ring for free after it's presented. That said, whether your proposal is going to be a surprise or not, there are multiple ways you can make a close estimate of your girlfriend's ring size. The very best way to do this is to measure your girlfriend's ring finger using a professional ring sizer (available from virtually any jeweler or jewelry store, or free by mail from BlueNile.com at *http://ringsize. bluenile.com*). You can also create your own ring sizer using a strip of paper.

To create your own ring sizer, cut a strip of paper that's no more than 3/4 of an inch wide. You can also use a piece of string. Wrap the paper strip or string around the base of the appropriate finger where the ring will be worn. Using a pen, mark the point on the strip of paper or string where it overlaps around the finger, thus forming a complete circle. The paper strip or string should have two marks—where the circle starts and ends. Next, use a ruler to accurately measure the length between the two marks on the paper or string. This will be you the circumference of the finger.

Ring Sizes (Based on U.S. Standards)	
Finger Circum-ference	Ring Size
43.4mm	3
44.9	3.5
46.5	4
47.8	4.5
49	5
50.3	5.5
51.5	6
52.8	6.5
54	7
55.3	7.5
56.6	8
57.8	8.5
59.1	9
60.3	9.5
61.6	10
62.8	10.5
64.1	11
65.3	11.5
66.6	12
67.9	12.5
69.1	13

Using the chart on page 30, you can determine the correct ring size, but it's obviously more accurate to have a professional jeweler use a ring sizer to measure your girlfriend's finger. As you're measuring, make sure her finger is warm (because the size of her finger will vary based upon its temperature) and allow ample room to slide the ring over her knuckle.

If you can "borrow" one of your girlfriend's other rings, you can take it to the jeweler and have it measured. Just make sure the ring you use to obtain a measurement for the engagement ring is typically worn on the same finger and fits properly.

Where to Start Your Search

One of the best ways to begin your quest to find and purchase the perfect engagement ring is to solicit the advice of those around you who have already been through this process. Learn from the experience of friends and relatives and avoid making the same mistakes they might have made.

Next, and more importantly, find and visit at least three well-established online or traditional jewelers, then begin to develop relationships, see what's available, ask questions, conduct research, and acquire your own knowledge.

As you determine the types of rings you and your girlfriend like and establish your price range, start narrowing down ring designs and diamond shapes. Only after you've found the perfect ring, that you believe is within your price range, should you begin to negotiate price and financing options.

After you've visited a handful of jewelers, you will eventually need to choose one to work with and to make your purchase from. According to the Jewelers of America

(JA), just some of the questions you should ask your jeweler include:

- Is the jeweler one of the more than 10,000 members of Jewelers of America? Members follow the standards, conduct and business ethics outlined by the organization.

- How long has the jeweler been in business?

- What is the jeweler's reputation? You might want to contact your local Chamber of Commerce or Better Business Bureau to determine if the jeweler you plan to work with is reputable, even if you found that jeweler through a personal referral.

- What services are offered by the jeweler? In the years to come, will this jeweler be available to resize, clean, or remount the engagement ring?

- What is the jeweler's return policy? If you return the ring, will you receive a cash refund or store credit? What time period do you have to return the ring?

- Does the jeweler offer periodic sales? Are you being offered the lowest sale price for the engagement ring you're about to purchase?

- Will the jeweler spend time to educate you about buying a diamond engagement ring and answer all of your questions openly, honestly, and in a manner that you can easily understand?

- Are the diamonds offered by the jeweler certified by either the AGS or the GIA? If not, look elsewhere.

Getting Your Girlfriend's Input

Whether or not your soon-to-be fiancée will be involved in the engagement ring buying process is a personal decision. Most experts agree, however, that as the guy, it's vitally important to obtain a good understanding about the type and style of ring your girlfriend really wants. This can be done in many ways. For example, you could:

- Take your girlfriend engagement ring shopping before actually getting engaged and see first-hand the types of rings she likes. You don't need to have her with you to purchase the actual ring, but it's often helpful to get her input early on to ensure your purchase will make her truly happy.

- You can ask her friends and family members to subtly gather information on your behalf. At the very least, you'll want to know things like the diamond shape she'd prefer and what type of setting she'd like. It's also good to know about what jewelry she already owns, so you can potentially match the engagement ring.

- Observe the jewelry she wears. You might also want to peak into her jewelry box to develop a better understanding of her jewelry style and the type of metal (gold or platinum, for example) she prefers, so you can match the engagement ring.

- You can ask your girlfriend questions about the type of ring she'd want, "when and if" you were to propose.

- When you're hanging out together at home, you and your girlfriend can visit a Website, such as *www.adiamondisforever.com*, "just for fun," and have her create her own virtual ring.

-❀ Have one of her girlfriends subtly encourage her to design her own engagement ring online, than have her friend forward the design to you.

Even if she's involved in the ring selection process, you can still maintain the element of surprise in terms of your proposal by controlling when and how you ultimately pop the question (and how you present the ring to her). Much more information on how to actually propose follows in the next few chapters of this book.

Engagement and Commitment Ring Options for Same-Sex Couples

At the time of this writing, a few states offer a legal status, called a *civil union*, for same-sex couples, although this classification doesn't offer all of the same legal rights a married couple would receive. While same-sex partnerships are viewed and treated differently from state to state, and even more so from country to country, the fact remains that there are a tremendous number of gay and lesbian couples who are involved in loving and committed relationships.

For same-sex couples looking to formalize their relationship by participating in some type of commitment ceremony, getting formally engaged is an important first step. Thus, virtually all of the proposal ideas discussed in this book also apply to same-sex couples. As for the "rules" and "traditions" surrounding engagement rings, commitment rings, and wedding bands, many same-sex couples choose to follow their own hearts and create their own traditions.

PrideBride.com reports:

> *We suggest the wedding or commitment ring
> go on the right hand ring finger. To us, this
> indicates that we are together, but still distinct
> from the heterosexual crowd. It would be great
> if the tradition our generation started was that
> the gay wedding ring is on the right hand.*

When it comes to buying a diamond ring, or a gold or platinum band, the information offered throughout this chapter applies. However, another common type of metal used to create rings is titanium, which is more common for men's rings. Some of the companies mentioned later in this section offer lines of titanium commitment rings for same-sex couples. (Titanium is also typically cheaper than 18k gold, white gold, or platinum—perhaps a sensible consideration when purchasing a *pair* of rings.)

According to Titanium Era (*www.titaniumera.com*), an online jewelry store offering a wide variety of custom-made titanium rings for men and women:

> *Titanium is a lustrous, grey, metallic element
> used principally to make lightweight, resistant
> alloys. It is one of the transitional elements of the
> periodic table and has many desirable proper-
> ties, most notably its incredible strength and
> durability.*

There is a wide range of possible scenarios when it comes to same-sex couples exchanging engagement rings, commitment rings, or wedding bands. The following are just a few possibilities:

- ❧ At the time a man or woman proposes the idea of formalizing the relationship, an engagement ring can be presented to his or her partner. The person who is doing the proposing has the option to purchase an identical ring for him- or herself, or the significant other can later purchase an engagement ring for the person who did the proposing.

-❧ Both partners can exchange rings once they agree to formalize their relationship. These rings can be identical in style, or different. It's a matter of personal preference and what the rings symbolize to each person.

-❧ Instead of giving an engagement ring during the proposal process, the couple can purchase matching bands to be exchanged during their commitment or marriage ceremony.

No matter who presents the ring, the important thing is that the ring or rings you choose are beautiful symbols of the love and commitment you have for one another. Because there are no rules or traditions relating to engagement or commitment rings for same-sex couples, the ring(s) you choose should showcase your personal style and taste.

For women, engagement ring and wedding band styles are already well-established. For men, however, there are many male-oriented ring designs available that can be used as engagement or commitment rings. The tradition that a diamond engagement ring be presented as part of a proposal doesn't have to apply, although there are many beautiful traditional and contemporary ring styles that incorporate diamonds for both men and women.

To create rings that have extra meaning, one common practice is for same-sex couples to work with a jeweler to custom design their own engagement and/or commitment rings. However, many jewelry companies offer a number of rings suitable for same-sex couples looking to formalize their relationship.

In some situations, gay men choose traditional wedding bands as their engagement rings. Because finding stylish rings for men is sometimes difficult, consider browsing the many styles available from jewelers with Websites, as opposed to simply visiting local jewelry stores. In addition to the companies listed in this chapter, you can also use such search phrases as "commitment rings," "wedding bands," or "men's rings," on any Internet search engine (such as *Yahoo.com* or *Google.com*).

Choosing the perfect engagement or commitment ring(s) is an important decision, and you'll want to be comfortable shopping for your ring(s). As in many cases, visiting retail jewelry stores or working personally with a jeweler has its advantages. On the other hand, surfing the Internet to find and purchase your ring(s) offers a large and often more diverse selection of rings to choose from, plus the convenience of shopping online at any time of the day.

Whether you're visiting a jeweler in person or shopping online, it's important to find a highly reputable jewelry dealer with which you're comfortable working. Some couples might prefer to find a specifically gay-owned or gay-friendly jewelry store in their area for a more thorough selection, however, many stores and jewelers are more than happy to accommodate special requests and help you find just what you're looking for.

When shopping online, always be sure to inquire about the company's return and exchange policies before making your purchase. Make sure you know the address of the company and verify its phone number. Also, as soon as you receive your ring(s), have them appraised to ensure you've received what you've paid for (as well as for insurance purposes). It's also a good idea to pay for your online purchases with a major credit card (as opposed to a debit card, money order, money transfer service, cash, or personal check). As a last resort, you can always do a credit card chargeback if the jeweler and your purchase don't live up to expectations and you have difficulty obtaining a refund.

Because finding a good selection of engagement rings, commitment rings, or wedding rings that are suitable for men is often challenging, the following Websites showcase jewelry retailers that offer excellent selections in both traditional and more contemporary styles:

- ☙ BlueNile.com (800-242-2728, *www.bluenile. com*) offers a platinum men's diamond band, which features seven round diamonds enveloped in a platinum channel. This band has a rounded inside edge for comfortable wear and offers a total diamond weight of 1/2 carat. Price: $1,700 (item number 1118). BlueNile.com also has an extensive collection of traditional solid gold or platinum wedding bands.

- ☙ TeNo (800-360-2586, *www.TenoUSA.com*) offers an extensive selection of titanium men's and women's rings (many incorporating diamonds and other jewels) in contemporary designs. TeNo (pronounced *teeno*) also offers a unique selection of "partnership rings" for same-sex couples.

- ☙ PlatinumJewels.com (888-656-6564, *www. platinumjewels.com*) offers a large selection of diamond rings, as well as platinum and titanium bands designed for men, any of which could be used by a same-sex couple as their engagement, commitment, or wedding rings.

- ☙ Moonstone Jewelry (800-557-4583, *www. moonstone-jewelry.com*) offers a selection of more traditional gold and platinum bands (some incorporating diamonds and other jewels), plus a line of "gay and lesbian lover rings." The company's "lover's knot" ring, combining gold and silver, serves as a beautiful symbol of love.

-❦ Titanium Rings Studio (775-827-9777, *www. tirings.com*) features a large selection of gold, platinum, and titanium rings for men, some of which incorporate diamonds and other jewels.

-❦ E-Weddingbands.com (800-291-9559, *www. e-weddingbands.com*) offers more traditional wedding bands for men in gold, white gold, titanium, and platinum.

As someone involved in a same-sex relationship, if you are interested in popping the question to your significant other and incorporating the presentation of a ring into that proposal, you'll want to find a perfect ring that symbolizes your love and commitment. And just like heterosexual couples, you'll want to develop and implement a proposal scenario that's memorable, romantic, and special for you both.

[For additional information about same-sex marriages, an organization called GLAD (Gay and Lesbian Advocate Defenders) offers a free, 45-page document, called *Civil Marriage for Same-Sex Couples: the Facts*, which can be downloaded from *www.glad.org/Publications/CivilRightProject/ CivilMarriage_TheFacts.PDF*.]

Appraisals and Insurance

Why is protecting your purchase with insurance important? The U.S. Department of Justice has estimated that jewelry accounts for as much as 70 percent of all stolen property, with more than $1 billion worth of jewelry disappearing each year.

As soon as you've made your ring purchase, it's an excellent idea to seek out an independent jewelry appraiser—preferably one who is not also a jewelry *retailer*—and have the ring appraised for insurance purposes. Next, obtain the necessary insurance to protect the ring against loss, theft, or damage. There are many insurance companies in the United States and worldwide that offer stand-alone Personal Jewelry Insurance policies. Many jewelers offer their own insurance programs by working in conjunction with insurance companies. Just as you insure your other valuables, such as your home, personal belongings, and automobile, it's an excellent idea to insure your expensive jewelry, such as your engagement ring (and eventually your wedding bands).

According to Jewelers Mutual Insurance Company (800-558-6411, *www.jewelersmutual.com*), one of the leading insurers of jewelry in America:

> *The annual premium for your Personal Jewelry Insurance policy is determined by the retail replacement value of each item of jewelry you insure. The rates vary according to the value of each item and according to your state or country of residence. Rates start as low as $1 per $100 of value, with no deductible. Optional deductible choices are available that allow for premium credits. For example, if the jewelry item you wish to insure is valued at $5,000 and the rate for the state in which you reside is $1 per $100, the annual premium you would pay would be $50.*

Chubb Insurance Solutions (877-972-8282 or 888-862-4822, *www.chubbsolutions.com*) is another insurance company that offers Personal Jewelry Insurance. With a single phone call, Chubb Insurance Solutions can provide you with a quote and immediate coverage for all of your jewelry. As a general rule, the annual insurance premium will be between 1 percent and 3 percent of the purchase price of the jewelry.

Prior to purchasing a separate insurance policy for your engagement ring, determine what coverage is offered through your existing home owner's (or renter's) insurance policy. Many home owner's policies, however, limit jewelry coverage to as low as $1,000, and will only insure specific types of losses, which is why a separate personal jewelry insurance policy is usually recommended in order to protect your engagement ring and wedding band purchases. Keep in mind, in many states a jeweler cannot directly recommend how you should protect your jewelry purchase against loss, theft, or damage. Contact a licensed insurance broker or insurance company representative for more information.

Paying for Your Engagement Ring

If you're following the tradition of spending about two months' salary on an engagement ring, you're about to make a significant purchase. Based on your income, credit rating, employment, and overall financial situation, you have several options when it comes to paying for the ring, including:

- Paying in-full with cash (from savings, investments, etc.).

- Paying with a major credit card. (If you choose this option, choose a card that offers some type of reward, such as frequent flier miles for a major airline.)

- Financing the ring through the jeweler (if you qualify, based on your credit rating). Many jewelers offer flexible financing options to help meet your needs.

- Obtaining a personal or home equity loan from a bank or financial institution (if you qualify, based on your credit rating).

- Borrowing the money from family.

Before you start shopping for an engagement ring, determine approximately what you can afford and how the ring will be paid for. If you hope to take out a loan or finance the ring, it's important that you know your credit rating and are confident you'll be able to obtain the financing you want and need.

As with any major purchase, if you choose to finance the engagement ring, look for the best deals possible in terms of interest rates and payback period. Also, determine what monthly payments you can realistically afford, based on your current financial situation.

Finally, if you're considering taking advantage of a jeweler's financing program, beware of special financing offers that are too good to be true. Always read all of the fine print and understand the offer being made before you accept it. If you're offered 60, 90, 120, or more days with no interest or payments, determine how the interest will be accrued and calculated after that initial period. Just as if you're applying for a major credit card, make sure you know the Annual Percentage Rate (interest rate) and all of the other fees associated with obtaining the financing. The worse your credit rating, the higher the interest rate you can expect to pay, if you get accepted for the financing at all. Always read the fine print carefully!

Simply by shopping around for the best financing deal, you could easily save hundreds, perhaps thousands, of dollars in interest payments over the term of the loan (financing). It may make sense to obtain an additional credit card with a lower interest rate than what the jeweler's financing program offers in order to make your purchase. You can research various credit card offers by visiting these free Websites:

- Bank Rates, *www.bankrate.com.*

- Card Locator, *www.cardlocator.com.*

- Card Offers: The Credit Card Directory, *www.cardoffers.com.*

- The Credit Card Catalog, *www. creditcardcatalog.com.*

- CreditLand, *www.credit-land.com.*

- Credit Cards Plus, *www.credit-cards-plus.com.*

To obtain a copy of your credit report, obtain your credit score, and determine, in advance, whether or not you'll qualify to finance an engagement ring, contact the following three credit bureaus:

- Equifax
  P.O. Box 740241
  Atlanta, GA 30374-0241
  800-685-1111
  https://www.econsumer.equifax.com/webapp/ ConsumerProducts/index.jsp

-❧ Experian (TRW)
  P.O. Box 2002
  Allen, TX 75013
  888-EXPERIAN
  www.experian.com

-❧ Trans Union
  P.O. Box 1000
  Chester, PA 19022
  900-916-8800
  www.transunion.com

Advice From the Experts

You've probably figured out by now that, for someone who isn't a professional jeweler or trained gemologist, buying a diamond can be a confusing experience. After all, next to buying a home or automobile, for example, this is probably one of the larger purchases you'll make in your lifetime, in terms of the amount of money you're about to spend. Remember, a diamond engagement ring should not be purchased as a financial investment. It's a symbol of love and should be purchased as a sentimental object of beauty and radiance with the idea that it will become a family heirloom.

To help you make the right decisions when selecting a diamond engagement ring, the following are interviews with experts from well-known jewelry companies, including the world-famous Harry Winston and Bluenile.com.

What you're about to read are the opinions of experienced individuals. In some cases, the opinions offered about specific topics differ. Use this information to help you make your own educated decisions and formulate your own thoughts and opinions relating to the diamond engagement ring selection and buying process.

Jim Haag
Vice President of Marketing and Sales, Harry Winston

718 Fifth Avenue   317 North Rodeo Drive
New York, NY 10019   Beverly Hills, CA 90210
212-245-2000   310-271-8554

(Additional locations in Geneva, Paris, Tokyo, and Osaka.)
www.harry-winston.com

Harry Winston is probably one of the most famous jewelers in the world? How did the company obtain this reputation?

Jim: Harry Winston, as a company, is more than 115 years old. It was founded by Harry's father, Jacob Winston, who established the company in the late 1800s under a different name. Harry later began working with his father in Los Angeles. As the story goes, when Harry was 12 years old, he went to a garage sale and purchased a piece of green glass for a quarter. He brought it home and showed it to his father. It turned out to be an emerald which he later resold for $800. From that point on, it was discovered that Harry Winston had an instinct for gems. When Harry was in his 20s, he moved to New York and made a reputation for himself by buying jewelry from famous estates. This was in the early part of the 1900s. At the time, the jewelry, which had often been created in the 1800s, had a lot of heavy metal on it. Harry broke up all of the jewelry and remade it, to get rid of the excessive metal. He thought metal wrapped around gemstones impeded the sparkle and brilliance of the stones. Thus, he developed a whole new way of setting the stones in jewelry. It was almost an invisible setting.

By acquiring jewelry from some of the most famous estates of his time and remaking the jewelry from those collections, Harry Winston developed his early reputation. In 1934, he purchased a 726 carat rough diamond, called the Jonker Diamond, which he cut into 11 diamonds. The Jonker Diamonds became very famous in film clips in the 1930s. In 1949, Harry Winston acquired the famous Hope Diamond from the estate of Evalyn Walsh McLean for more than $1 million. By coordinating a series of jewel exhibitions for charity, more than $10 million was raised by Harry Winston for various charities over a 10-year period between the 1940s and 1950s. It was his dream to establish a national gem collection, which was ultimately created in 1958, when he donated the Hope Diamond to The Smithsonian Museum. Today, the Hope Diamond has a value of more than $200 million, and is one of the most viewed museum objects in the world.

It was the acquisition of famous stones and estate jewelry collections that initially put Harry Winston on the map. It was in 1943 that celebrities started borrowing famous jewels to wear to the Oscar Awards. This was a process and tradition that Harry Winston began. It continues to this day.

Harry Winston ran his company until he died in 1978. It was then taken over by his son, Ronald Winston. Harry Winston remains a privately held company.

Obviously, Harry Winston caters to extremely famous and wealthy clientele. What about ordinary people, with average incomes, who want to purchase an engagement ring?

Jim: We do a lot of business with couples about to get married, who are between the ages of 20 and 30, for example. These are people first starting off in their careers, who aren't necessarily wealthy, but who have good earning potential. Our engagement rings start at one carat, with prices starting between $12,000 and $14,000. This is not totally out of the price range of many people. Our prices for engagement rings are about the same as most upscale jewelers in New York City, for example.

What's the best way to start the search for the perfect engagement ring?

Jim: What the soon-to-be groom is searching for is an engagement ring that will fulfill the dreams of his girlfriend. I recommend that the girlfriend be involved in the selection of the ring's design—in terms of the diamond's shape and cut, for example. Usually, about 60 percent of the time, the couple will shop together for their ring before they actually get engaged. This is when the couple will passively look at ring designs and styles. It's common for the ring shopping process to begin six months to a full year before the engagement. Think of this as a journey. It's a journey that should take you to several different jewelers in an effort to gather information over time. Once the couple narrows down their search, the guy will typically return to their jeweler of choice alone and purchase the ring. By initially shopping around together, the man knows what the woman is looking for and has more confidence in what he's buying. In this situation, the guy is more apt to buy a finer piece of jewelry than if he's shooting in the dark about the type of ring his future fiancée wants.

What is the best way to gather information about diamonds and engagement rings?

Jim: For many guys, buying an engagement ring is one of their first really big purchases in their lives. Most guys feel they need to do their homework before they start shopping and visiting jewelry stores. At Harry Winston, we have people whose grandfather and father both bought their engagement rings from us, so the son comes to us as the first and only jeweler he visits. Guys should come into a jewelry store with a general knowledge about diamonds and rings, however, most jewelers will be happy to offer a free education to the customer. It's good to have some knowledge, but you must also trust the expert jeweler you ultimately select and rely on his knowledge. Some guys feel they have to have too much knowledge. Thus, they focus too much on the technical aspects of buying a diamond. These people sometimes miss the fact that buying a diamond isn't just a science. It's also an art. The consumer needs to open his eyes and look at the stone itself and love it. You can't just look at the certification form or find a stone that meets a certain description when buying an engagement ring.

The final criteria about which diamond to purchase should be based upon what the purchaser thinks is beautiful. Guys should know that a woman will often look at three round diamonds that are the same quality, for example, but one of those diamonds will always jump out at her. There's no real rational reason for this, aside from the fact that one diamond is more beautiful than the other two *to her*. Guys need to use the technical information they acquire about diamonds as a guideline for their purchase, but not necessarily as the final decision criteria.

What other advice about buying a diamond for an engagement ring can you share?

Jim: I always recommend that people buy a diamond based on *quality* rather than *size*. There are several reasons for this. A quality stone will have a higher intrinsic specialness and will often increase in value faster than a lesser quality stone. A better quality stone is also usually prettier and has a better cut on it. Harry Winston always believed that it was the quality of the stone that is important. That's an idea we continue to promote.

Should someone look at the purchase of a diamond engagement ring as a financial investment?

Jim: Yes and no. People should never buy a diamond because it's a good investment. They should buy a diamond because it's a beautiful work of art and a symbol of love. Diamonds have historically increased in value over time, so they tend to be a good financial investment as well—although it's a long-term proposition.

What are some of the important decisions a buyer needs to make?

Jim: One of the biggest decisions relating to the purchase of an engagement ring is selecting the right jeweler to work with. Look for a jeweler, not just a jewelry store. The relationship you develop with your jeweler should last for many years to come. Most people have a tax accountant, hairdresser, doctor, stock broker, and fitness trainer, for example. They also need a jeweler. Over the course of your marriage, as a couple, you'll be buying more jewelry. The jeweler can assist you in buying pieces in the future that will improve and round out your collection. Many people, without a relationship with their jeweler, will buy a series of mismatched jewelry pieces during their marriage.

When you're acquiring a jewelry wardrobe that starts with your engagement ring, you can build a set of jewelry that has a real special value to it. For your 10th anniversary, for example, you might buy a random piece of jewelry. Another option is to purchase a necklace, bracelet, or earrings, for example, that perfectly coordinate with the diamond engagement ring. A jeweler will help you plan your jewelry purchases to help you buy the best pieces. Over the course of your marriage, you'll likely spend upwards of $50,000 or more on jewelry. After the acquisitions, you want to wind up with a collection that's valuable. Your jeweler can help you with this and provide you with a lot of great advice in the years to come.

Won't purchasing an engagement ring from an upscale jeweler be more expensive?

Jim: There are two reasons to work with a well-established jeweler with a top-notch reputation. First, you could buy from a discount jewelry store, for example, but you won't wind up saving too much money, especially if you buy a loose diamond and then need to have it mounted. In the years to come, you'll want your jeweler to adjust and maintain the ring, alter its size, make adjustments if the stone becomes loose, and maybe change the setting. These are things your jeweler will do for you that a discount jeweler might not.

What makes the perfect engagement ring?

Jim: It's all about what the woman wants. This should be a ring that fulfills her every desire and fantasy. The guy is filling the role of hero by buying her something fabulous. For the guy, he's buying the emotional reward of her receiving this ring. You need to buy the ring that the woman wants. That's the perfect ring. This is an emotional purchase. On a rational level, the perfect ring is one that you believe you're getting a good value on, in terms of quality for money spent. You need to walk out of the jeweler believing the ring you purchased was worth the money you paid for it. Finding this "perfect ring" will take a lot of legwork. As the guy, you have to determine what it is the woman wants, even if she doesn't tell you outright.

The woman always has concerns and fears about the major changes about to happen in her life relating to getting married, starting a family, perhaps buying a house, and later having children. I have found that the man usually wants to spend more than the woman for an engagement ring. The guy needs to try to read the subtle clues about what the woman really wants, because this is a ring that could be on her finger for the next 50 years or more. Five, 10, or 20 years down the road, you won't remember how much you spent on the ring, nor will you really care. Over the years, I have seen many brides come back with regrets that they didn't initially purchase the stone they really wanted in terms of size or quality. This is a long-term proposition. I recommend that the guy develop an understanding of what the woman really wants, not just what she's saying she wants. I recommend getting the ring *now* that you and she really want.

In terms of finding that perfect ring, how important are such things as the setting, quality of the diamond, timelessness of the design, the comfort, the craftsmanship, the warranty, and the finance options available?

Jim: Number one is the quality of the stone and the stone itself. Ninety percent of the value of the ring relates directly to the main diamond. You have to absolutely love the diamond. Everything else is secondary. A jeweler can always change the mounting of the ring in a matter of days, for example. Focus on the stone!

The second most important thing is the timelessness of the design. Some women come in and say they want something modern, for example, but you need to consider what you and other people will think of the design 10 or 15 years from now. You want something that looks classic and timeless now and in the future.

Third, look for the uniqueness of the ring. Every woman wants something that nobody else has. They want something that is a little bit different—not a ring they know their neighbor down the street also has. The cut of the diamond, the shape of the diamond, and the setting could be different.

The fourth thing to consider is your comfort in the price you pay. No couple wants to spend too much or outside of what they can realistically afford. You don't want to overstretch your finances to purchase the ring. It's up to the guy to be the hero and determine how the ring will ultimately be paid for. It's his "job" to pick the perfect ring and make sure he can afford it. A good jeweler will work with you to determine the right price point for you. Remember, the right jeweler will want to develop a long-term relationship with you. If they make you spend too much on this ring, you won't feel comfortable coming back.

As for the payment plans and the rest of the things to consider, they're important, but shouldn't be the deciding factor. A company like Harry Winston will help the customer create a customized payment plan they're comfortable with.

In terms of the ring's setting, what should someone consider—white gold, 18-karat gold, or platinum?

Jim: We always recommend platinum for rational and emotional reasons. Platinum is a more precious metal. The better quality diamonds are always mounted in platinum, unless the customer wants a yellow metal. In that case, go with 18-karat yellow gold. Out of 100 engagement rings we sell, only one will be in white gold. Platinum is a harder substance with stronger prongs to hold the diamond in place. It's also a more illustrious metal and is more durable. Platinum will hold up better and longer than gold.

Why is the whole engagement ring buying process so confusing?

Jim: One reason is because the guy and the girl are still getting to know each other prior to getting engaged, yet they're spending a pretty good amount of money on this single purchase. He's trying to get her what she really wants, while she is trying to figure out what he really wants to spend. There's rarely an open line of communication between the couple. There's a lot of self-esteem issues and worry that they won't do the right thing relating to this particular buying decision. The guy is worried he won't spend enough money, not get the right stone, and that she isn't going to love the ring. The woman is worried about asking for too much or that he'll spend too much. There's a whole emotional dynamic going on.

Also, there's a pressure on the guy to buy the right stone, which often results in him trying to over-educate himself about diamonds and precious metals. There's a difference between educating yourself and overeducating yourself. You should rely on and trust your jeweler because he or she will already have this knowledge. I have seen people come in to look at our diamonds with pages and pages of notes and charts in their hands. They evaluate the specifications of the diamond, but never actually look at the diamond itself. That's a mistake. Don't get too into or lost in the technical part of the buying decision.

When it comes to buying an engagement ring, you have many choices. You can visit a local jeweler in your town or city; find a chain jewelry store at a local mall; buy from a well-known, upscale jeweler, such as Harry Winston or Tiffany & Co.; or shop online and get the same top quality diamond ring in an 18-karat gold or platinum setting, but save a fortune.

Founded in May 1999, BlueNile.com has "married" more than 35,000 couples from across the United States through its innovative, extremely informative, and highly functional Website. Combining the latest Web-based technologies with top-notch customer service and telephone sales support, Blue Nile offers only the highest quality diamonds and fine jewelry, without any pressure from pushy or commission-based salespeople. You can spend as much time as you want exploring and learning from the company's Website, then get your questions answered by an expert over the telephone or online.

Blue Nile offers the convenience of being able to shop for an engagement ring 24 hours a day from the comfort of your computer at home or at work. At the same time, you can receive anywhere from 20 to 40 percent off traditional retail prices on diamond engagement rings, plus choose from an inventory of more than 21,000 certified diamonds and more then 70 different settings. Best of all, you can see exactly what you're getting on the computer screen, using the company's innovative "Build Your Own Ring" feature, then have the exact ring you're looking for delivered anywhere in the United States, within five business days.

To ensure that customers receive the engagement ring they truly want, anyone who isn't 100-percent satisfied with their purchase can return it for an exchange or full refund within 30 days. As the leading online-based retailer of diamonds in America, Blue Nile has developed a reputation for offering the finest quality at outstanding prices.

As you're exploring Blue Nile's Website, highly trained diamond consultants can be reached by phone, Monday through Friday, between 8 a.m. and midnight (EST), and on Saturdays and Sundays, between 9 a.m. and 10 p.m. (EST). Around holidays, such as Christmas, Mother's Day, and Valentine's Day, the company's hours are extended.

With more than 100 employees, Blue Nile has quickly become one of the largest retailers of diamonds and fine jewelry in the country. As the Director of Diamond Merchandizing for Blue Nile, Brian Watkins manages the nation's largest collection of high quality, independently certified diamonds. In this interview, he shares his valuable experience.

Brian Watkins
Director of Diamond Merchandizing,
Blue Nile, Inc.

Seattle, WA
888-565-7610
www.bluenile.com

Why was BlueNile.com created, and why, despite the disappearance of so many other Internet companies, has Blue Nile become so successful with continued record growth each year?

Brian: Blue Nile was created to help confused and stressed guys make one of the most important and emotional purchases of their lives—the diamond engagement ring. The inspiration for the company came from the personal experience of our founder and CEO, Mark Vadon. Like millions of guys before him, Mark was searching for the perfect engagement ring. He wanted to find a ring that would sweep his girlfriend off her feet, but as he went through the process, he became confused and overwhelmed.

While visiting a local jewelry store in San Francisco, the salesman put two rings in front of him. One was about $10,000 and the other was around $15,000. As he looked at the rings, he realized he couldn't tell the difference between the two. Mark had this perception that while he knew nothing about diamonds, the woman he'd be giving the ring to knew a lot, and he didn't want to disappoint her or look stupid.

As a result, Mark decided to start over. He started doing research online to educate himself about this big, important purchase. During his research, he talked to friends who had been through this same process, and discovered he wasn't alone. Most guys don't understand what they're buying, and because it's such an emotional purchase, the entire process is pretty stressful.

His experience, coupled with the feedback from friends, led to the creation of Blue Nile. The company's goal is to simplify the engagement ring buying process by empowering the customer with tons of educational information in a no-pressure atmosphere so the customer is the one in charge of the process. Then we back it up with great customer service and the highest quality diamonds and fine jewelry at prices 20 to 40 percent below retail.

I think Blue Nile has been so successful because we're answering a consumer need. At some point in life, most guys are going to get engaged, but they aren't comfortable with the traditional engagement ring purchasing process. We created a radically different way to find and purchase the engagement ring that puts the guy in charge of the process, and consumers have really responded. In fact, the biggest reason for the continued growth of our company is because of referrals. We do very little advertising. People just like what we offer and tell their friends.

Who is the target customer for Blue Nile? Do you cater to people in a specific income bracket or people who are extremely computer savvy?

Brian: Our customer is any guy looking for that perfect engagement ring, but who's uncomfortable with the traditional process. Four years ago, our customer was

a computer-savvy, youngish male, but now people are
so familiar with the Internet that we have customers
from all age groups. You don't need to be a computer
whiz to use our site and obtain free information
about diamond buying.

**What does Blue Nile offer that a traditional retail
jeweler doesn't offer? What are the benefits and draw-
backs of selecting and buying a diamond engagement
ring from your company?**

Brian: I think you can sum up the benefit of shopping at
Blue Nile with one word: *empowerment.* At Blue Nile,
the customer controls every step of the process.

Consumers can shop for as long as they want,
from home or work, day or night, without any pressure
or hovering salespeople. Without having to ask a salesperson the right questions, or relying on that person
to provide you with accurate answers, consumers can
learn everything they need to know about buying a
diamond using the diamond education section of
our Website.

When it comes to selection, even a large jewelry
store will have, at most, a few hundred diamonds;
visitors to our site can select from more than 21,000
high quality diamonds, independently certified by
either the GIA or AGS.

Consumers can also design the diamond ring according to their specifications, see how it looks, and
purchase it right from our Website. We'll build it and
then ship it via FedEx to you in about five days.

If you need additional help, you'll find our atti-
tude is also very different from a typical salesperson
at a jewelry store. When someone calls our toll-free
number, our mission is not to *sell* the person, but

find the perfect diamond based on their personal specifications and budget. We offer guidance, with absolutely no sales pressure. In fact, it's quite common for us to recommend a less expensive option to a customer than the one he had in mind, if we think it's a better value or a better match to the customer's criteria.

When someone goes to a jewelry store in person, they can see the exact diamond they're buying. This isn't possible when shopping online. Is that a drawback when trying to find the perfect engagement ring?

Brian: There's a misconception that you need to see a diamond in order to understand what you're buying. I could put two very different diamonds in front of you, with very different prices, and 99 percent of the time you won't be able to tell which is the better diamond. How, then, does seeing the diamond help?

Most people don't know it, but professional diamond buyers for major jewelry chains rarely, if ever, actually see the diamonds they buy. They make their purchase based on information—on the four Cs—and that's what we teach our customers to do. Once you understand how a diamond is graded, and what that means to you as the buyer, our Website allows you to go through each of the four Cs and find a certified diamond that meets your criteria and budget.

What we find is that because our customers understand what they're buying, they're much more likely to be satisfied with their purchase than customers who see and touch the diamond. That's why our return rate for diamond engagement rings is much lower than the industry average. In fact, the number-one reason engagement rings are returned to Blue Nile is because she declined the proposal.

We encourage people to compare quality and prices between what we offer and any other jeweler. We also encourage our customers to call our expert consultants as often as they need, to ensure that their questions are answered and their concerns are addressed.

How do the prices at Blue Nile differ from what you'd find at regular jewelry stores or upscale stores, such as Harry Winston or Tiffany & Co.? How does the quality of your merchandise differ?

Brian: Generally speaking, Blue Nile customers can expect to save between 20 to 40 percent, compared to the prices at physical jewelry retailers. The quality and craftsmanship of our diamond engagement rings is equal to or better than what you'll find at even the most celebrated jewelry stores. The quality of stones at Blue Nile is consistent with the most prestigious names in the industry.

Our platinum settings, for example, are 95 percent platinum, which is the highest grade possible. Even our gold engagement rings are secured with platinum heads to improve their strength and preserve the colorlessness of the diamond.

Buying a diamond online can be something some consumers are leery of. Thus, we adhere to an extremely high standard and work hard to exceed customers' expectations.

What should people do as they begin searching for the perfect engagement ring?

Brian: The first thing someone needs to do is establish a budget for themselves. The tradition of spending two or three months' salary on the engagement ring should be thrown out the window. You need to consider what you can afford and what you feel comfortable with.

Next, think about the specifications of the diamond and the ring that are important to you and your girlfriend. For example, do you want an absolutely flawless diamond? Are you willing to drop down a step in color, for example, to buy a better diamond in terms of clarity?

The whole process is a lot like buying a car. You first decide on the style of car you want, then pick and choose the various options. When it comes to a diamond, select the cut and the shape first. Next, start playing around with color, clarity, and carat, based on your price limit.

Never be pushed into a diamond purchase that you can't afford or that you're not comfortable with. You should never feel like you're being taken advantage of. Don't allow a fast-talking salesperson to force you into something you don't like or can't afford.

Our customers tell us about salespeople using phrases like, "Choose the diamond that speaks to you," "It's not what you're buying, but why," or "Can you really put a price on love?" when what the customer needs is tangible advice they can use. Yes, you want to take her breath away, but putting a price on love is an ambiguous statement. It's a ploy some salespeople use to guilt you into spending more money.

Buying a diamond is an intellectual process that has several emotional components. You can protect yourself from getting ripped off or spending too much by focusing on the quantifiable aspects of your purchase. The act of proposing with the ring is the emotional component.

Keep in mind that within almost any realistic budget, you should be able to find a beautiful diamond engagement ring.

How do you define a perfect engagement ring?

Brian: I always advocate going with a better quality diamond than a larger size. A better quality diamond will be more beautiful, and have more of a "presence" than a larger diamond of inferior quality.

That said, cut should be your first consideration because it determines the diamond's brilliance and flash. In terms of color, many people are convinced they must have a colorless diamond, when in reality they can't tell the difference between a colorless [F-rated] and less expensive, near colorless [G-rated] diamond, for example. The clarity of the diamond is important. Thus, choose a diamond that is at least flawless to the naked eye. SI1-rated clarity, or better, is best.

In terms of finding that perfect ring, how important are such things as the setting, quality of the diamond, timelessness of the design, the comfort, the craftsmanship, the warranty, and the finance options available?

Brian: When it comes to the setting, consider your girlfriend's personality. Whether she's physically active and what she does for a living should impact your choice of settings. The other types of jewelry she often wears should also be considered when choosing the metal for the setting. Just based on your girlfriend's personality and habits, we can narrow down the perfect setting from over 70 to just a few. Then, it's a matter of personal taste. Some women want a trendy and modern design. I think that's perfectly fine, because 10 years down the road, you can always have the diamond refitted into a different setting rather inexpensively.

A lot of jewelers will use warranty as bait for why you should buy the ring from them. In reality, no matter where you purchase your ring, any reputable jeweler will later clean your ring and check the prongs for little or no money. What's far more important is making sure your ring is fully insured against theft, loss, or damage.

What should someone look for when financing their ring purchase?

Brian: Most jewelers offer several different financing options through a partner. Shop around for the best financing deals. A credit card may have a better rate than a finance company that's partnered with the jeweler you're working with.

At Blue Nile, we currently offer 90-days, "same as cash" financing and a 60-month financing plan. Some people apply for a new credit card to pay for the engagement ring. They find a credit card that offers frequent flier miles for a major airline as a reward for using that credit card. They then use those frequent flier miles to travel on their honeymoon. There are many different options relating to how to pay for the ring. These decisions should be based upon your personal financial situation and your credit rating. Whatever financing option you choose, read all of the fine print before jumping into anything.

At Blue Nile, we can take up to three different forms of payment for a single purchase, so you can put some of the purchase on a credit card and pay cash for the remaining balance, for example. For bank wire transfers, we offer a 1.5-percent discount on the purchase.

In terms of the ring's setting, what should someone consider—white gold, 18-karat gold, or platinum?

Brian: The difference between 18-karat yellow gold and platinum is a matter of personal preference. If it's between white gold and platinum, we always recommend platinum because it's much more durable. Platinum is a strong metal that will develop a patina over time that will hide any small scratches. There are several precautions you need to take when dealing with white gold. For example, you need to keep the ring away from harsh chemicals and cleaning supplies. White gold will also require more maintenance in the years to come. If you're choosing gold, use 18-karat for the band, because it offers the best combination of beauty and strength. We also use and recommend platinum fittings to hold the diamond in place, even for 18-karat gold settings.

What other diamond engagement ring buying advice can you offer?

Brian: A lot of guys are under the impression they should buy the biggest possible diamond, not the best quality. That's simply not the case. There's a phrase in this industry, called "buying shy," that can help you maximize your purchase. For example, because diamond prices jump at the carat and half-carat, if you buy a diamond that's just short of 1 carat, as opposed to exactly 1 carat, you'll achieve significant savings without a noticeable decrease in size.

One major piece of advice is don't wait until the last minute. This should not be a decision you rush. The last thing you need is to be in a state of panic about purchasing the right ring. The experience should be as stress-free as possible and based on educated buying decisions. Do your homework, shop around, and find a deal and a jeweler you're comfortable with. Never compromise what you want based on the inventory a particular jeweler has on hand when you're ready to make your purchase.

Finally, make absolutely sure the diamond you're buying is certified by the GIA or AGS. Never simply take the word of a jeweler about a diamond's rating or grade. Demand proof in the form of certification from one of these two internationally recognized and respected certification labs.

Should someone get their ring appraised immediately after they make their purchase to ensure they got what they paid for?

Brian: That's always a good idea. Just make sure you bring the ring and certification to an independent, licensed jewelry appraiser who has a gemology degree, not your local jewelry store. You want someone who will evaluate the diamond and the ring itself and tell you exactly what you've purchased and its value.

What tips can you offer for choosing a diamond engagement ring that's unique or one-of-a-kind?

Brian: We specialize in ring styles that are classic. Customers can choose from a variety of different diamond shapes, different metals, and from more than 70 different setting styles. Anyone can mix and match these elements to create a perfect personalized ring. From our Website, customers can experiment with these different elements and actually see the ring they design for themselves on their computer screen.

Other Valuable Resources

- ❧ **A Diamond Is Forever** (*www.adiamondisforever. com*)—You've probably seen their ads on TV and in magazines. This is a free information source about diamonds that's sponsored by the Diamond Trading Company, the world's leading diamond sales and marketing company. The Website is designed to educate consumers and boost their confidence in the diamond buying process. None of the jewelry featured is sold on the site. The pieces were all provided from various manufacturers across the United States.

- ❧ **American Gem Society** (800-341-6214, *www. ags.org*)—The American Gem Society was established in 1934. This is a well-known and internationally trusted independent gemological laboratory that grades and certifies diamonds to help determine their value. Among the services this organization offers is a referral service for finding a reputable jeweler when shopping for engagement rings. The organization's Website also offers extensive information about the diamond buying process.

- ❧ **Diamonds.com** (877-956-9600, *www. Diamonds.com*)—This Website offers an excellent "Education" section for choosing and purchasing a diamond engagement ring. The organization is sponsored by a network of jewelers and diamond specialists.

- ❧ **Gemological Institute of America** (800-421-7250, *www.gia.org*)—Like the American Gem Society, the Gemological Institute of America (GIA) is an independent gemological laboratory that grades and certifies diamonds. Respected industry-wide, the GIA was founded in Los Angeles in 1931 by Robert M. Shipley and offers educations in its expert knowledge of diamonds and gemstones. The International Diamond Grading System was created and introduced there by Richard T. Liddicoat in 1953, and the institute has grown to become the most respected grading and identification authority in the world.

- ❧ **Jewelers of America** (800-223-0673, *www.jewelers.org*)—This is a national association comprised of more than 10,000 jewelers nationwide. The organization offers a free referral service to help consumers locate reputable jewelers in their area.

Chapter 2

Traditional and Romantic Proposal Ideas

$\mathcal{O}$ kay, you've found the person of your dreams—someone with whom you'd like to potentially spend the rest of your life and perhaps someday build a family—and you've decided you'd like to propose marriage. Based upon the personalities of you both and your relationship together, chances are you want to pop the question in the most romantic and memorable way possible. This chapter is all about choosing and creating the perfect traditional and/or romantic method of proposing. Here, you'll find 26 marriage proposal ideas that can be customized to meet your particular needs. Hopefully, you'll find that this chapter and the next will help you tap into your own creativity and spark some ideas to help you pop the question.

Prior to choosing a method to propose, think about these questions:

- When will you pop the question? Is there a specific date, holiday, or season you have in mind?

- Will you take the traditional approach and ask your girlfriend's father for his permission to marry his daughter? If so, how and when will you take care of this formality?

- What type of proposal would you like to enact? Are you looking to be highly romantic and propose marriage in an intimate setting? Do you want this event to be experienced just between the two of you, or would you prefer something more public, extravagant, and fun?

- What type of marriage proposal has your girlfriend been dreaming about all of her life? What would it take to make her fantasy proposal a reality? Is she a traditional and romantic person, or would she appreciate you professing your love for her in front of a large crowd by popping the question in a very public place?

- Will you utilize the element of surprise when proposing?

- Where will the proposal take place? What will the location and setting be? What time of the day will you propose? If you're planning to pop the question during a sunset, for example, to help select the perfect time of day or night (and to best coordinate your planning), visit *http://aa.usno.navy.mil/data/docs/RS_OneDay.html* to help you determine the exact time of sunrise or sunset for any location, based on the date you enter.

- ❧ No matter what you plan to say, how you plan to say it, and where you plan to pop the question, will you incorporate the tradition of getting down on one knee into your proposal plan?

- ❧ What emotions, thoughts, and feelings do you want to convey as part of your proposal? Do you want to be funny, sincere, romantic, traditional, serious? How will you communicate these emotions and feelings (through your words and/or actions)?

- ❧ How much time and money do you have to invest in coming up with and executing your marriage proposal scenario?

The Perfect Proposal

The perfect wedding proposal is one that makes the couple's dreams come true. In some cases, it's about following tradition, reenacting a storybook-like scenario, or creating an event that will linger in your minds forever as being one of the happiest moments of your lives. It's about creating a moment when you actually commit your love and lives to one another and transform yourselves from being two single individuals into a soon-to-be-married couple.

Just as there is no perfect engagement ring that meets *everyone's* needs, there is no single perfect way to propose marriage. There are literally limitless options available to you in terms of what to say, how you say it, the location you select, and what actions you can take. While a book can suggest things to say and sentiments to communicate during your proposal, ultimately, your words must come directly from your own heart.

Gathering ideas for creating a fun, unique, memorable, romantic, or traditional marriage proposal situation is something you'll get from this book. Take these ideas and customize them to meet your needs. As you contemplate the perfect marriage proposal, it's absolutely vital that you consider the dreams, desires, fantasies, and personality of your girlfriend. After all, she's probably been dreaming about being proposed to since she was a little girl. It's now your job to live up to those fantasies and expectations by creating the romantic situation she has been dreaming about for a long time.

If you're a sports fan, for example, and you have dreamed about proposing in front of 35,000 fellow sports fans at a Major League Baseball game, that can be an awesome and memorable proposal (described in the next chapter). But if your girlfriend is very traditional and not into sports, this probably isn't the type of proposal scenario that would truly make *her* happy.

No matter how you propose, what you say, and what you do, hopefully your girlfriend will accept the proposal and you'll become engaged, making you both extremely happy. Your objective, however, should be to select and execute a marriage proposal that's romantic, memorable, and catered specifically to the person to whom you're proposing. Thus, planning is essential.

As a guy, the pressure to live up to expectations can be overwhelming in this situation. Assuming that you have selected the ideal woman for you to propose to (someone who loves you as much as you love her) and with whom you're truly compatible, consider putting the feelings you have into actions and words as part of your proposal. What you ultimately do to propose should be symbolic of the love, respect, and commitment you have for her.

Don't Get Caught at a Loss for Words

As the person about to propose marriage, what you say, how you say it, the location you choose, and the overall scenario you create are all equally important. Nobody can tell you exactly what to say or what sentiments you should convey during your actual proposal. Some people choose to make long speeches, and in the process, describe the history of the relationship, plus summarize all of the reasons why you two should be married. Others forego the speeches and simply create a mood, then quickly pop the question. Again, how you handle this should directly relate to the relationship you have, as well as the personalities and desires of both of you.

It's an excellent strategy to write out your proposal speech, memorize it, and rehearse it, to make sure it's perfect by the time you're actually ready to pop the question. If you're at a loss for words, consider the following questions. The answers should help you focus on what's important and what you'd like to say as you propose. (Remember, you can substitute "boyfriend" into any of the following questions to suit your situation.)

- Why is your girlfriend so special to you?
- What is it about your significant other that has captured your heart?
- What special qualities does your girlfriend possess?
- Why have you decided to propose now?
- What do you remember thinking the very first time you met? What was going through your head at the time?

- ❧ In what ways have your feelings evolved and grown since you first met?

- ❧ When did you first realize you were totally in love with your significant other? What happened to bring you to this realization?

- ❧ What are the five most loveable things about your girlfriend?

- ❧ What can and will you offer to your girlfriend to make her happy for the rest of her life (once you're married)?

- ❧ Knowing that once you get married, you could be spending the rest of your life together, what are you most looking forward to?

It's important to give serious thought to how and when you plan to propose, and then to invest the necessary time and energy to preplan the occasion. Even if you've discussed marriage many times in the past, you can still create a romantic element of surprise based on how and when you actually pop the question.

Let the Creativity Flow

Because there are 2.4 million weddings performed in the United States every single year, it's pretty difficult to conceive a totally unique and original method for proposing that hasn't been done before. What you can do, however, is take a marriage proposal ideal and totally customize it to make it your own.

As you develop your personal plan for how you'll pop the question, think about:

- What you will say—The ideas, thoughts, and emotions you wish to convey.

- How you will say it—What wording will you use?

- Location—Where will the proposal take place—your home, a restaurant, a party, the beach, or someplace that's sentimental (to one or both of you)?

- Environment and ambiance—Can you add music, candlelight, flowers, or other elements to create the perfect atmosphere?

- Timing—When will you pop the question? At sunset, after dinner, at a specific time of day or night?

- Who will be present—Aside from you and your significant other, who else will witness the proposal and/or help execute it?

- The preplanning involved—What needs to be done to ensure that the proposal you envision becomes a reality?

The rest of this chapter outlines more than two dozen marriage proposal ideas that are romantic, affordable, and relatively easy to implement. Many of these ideas are also somewhat traditional. To customize any of these ideas, be sure to add your own sentiments, choose the perfect timing, and communicate the feelings you have in your heart in the most romantic way possible. As you're about to discover, creating and executing the perfect wedding proposal idea doesn't necessarily have to cost a lot of money (except for the cost of the engagement ring, if you choose to be traditional and present a diamond ring, for example).

Once you've selected how and when you plan to pop the question, keep considering your girlfriend's point-of-view and how she'll react. Try to determine what she'll think of your proposal idea. Seek out advice or feedback from her family and friends—without letting your ideas get back to your girlfriend.

What a Tradition Proposal Involves

There's nothing wrong with any of the following traditions. However, when it comes to getting engaged, what's really important is what will make you and your significant other truly happy. If this means going against tradition, so be it. As you contemplate how your proposal will happen, consider these important steps:

- Ask your girlfriend's father for his permission and blessing to marry his daughter. This is a tradition, but not necessarily a requirement.

- Find and purchase the perfect engagement ring.

- Develop the perfect proposal scenario by choosing the best time and place, setting the right mood, and deciding exactly what you'll say and how you'll say it.

- Pop the question. This may or may not involve dropping to one knee and presenting a diamond engagement ring.

- Toast your engagement with champagne.

Traditional Marriage Proposal Ideas

If you're looking for outrageous, extravagant, or over-the-top marriage proposal ideas, check out the next chapter. The more traditional, affordable, and romantic ideas presented here are in no particular order. These ideas will help you create the perfect setting, ambiance, and mood to pop the question. Feel free to mix-and-match elements of these ideas to create your own proposal scenario that's perfect for you *and your girlfriend.*

Drop to One Knee and Propose (It's Ultra Traditional)

Proposal Concept: When with your girlfriend, get down on one knee, present an engagement ring, and propose marriage.

Approximate Scenario Cost: Free (except the cost of dinner if you choose a restaurant location)
  Plus the cost of the engagement ring.

Approximate Preparation Time: Minimal.

Supplies/Equipment Needed: The perfect location and an engagement ring.

Location: At home, at a restaurant, or any romantic location.

Related Contact Information/Resources: Not Applicable.

Forget all the hoopla, fanfare, and extravagance. This traditional proposal method is romantic and simply involves you and your girlfriend spending some quality time alone together—after a romantic dinner, before bed, on a nature walk, at the beach, or while on vacation, for example. You can pop the question virtually anywhere and anytime.

At the location that you decide is perfect, casually bring up how in love you are with your girlfriend and how wonderful it would be to spend the rest of your life with her. At just the right moment, get down on one knee, take her hand, present an engagement ring, and propose marriage.

This approach is simple, direct, and can be extremely romantic—especially if you combine the actions described here with some carefully selected words to convey your true feelings for her. Of course, you can use this traditional proposal method any day or night of the year. However, you might decide that a holiday, such as Valentine's Day, Christmas, New Year's Eve, her birthday, or some other date, is the perfect time for you to propose.

If you choose this proposal scenario, consider the environment and location where you'll be proposing. Add special touches, such as romantic music, roses, candlelight, or time your proposal perfectly with a sunset. Also, read through the rest of the proposal ideas described in this chapter to see if you want to combine multiple marriage proposal scenarios and ideas to create the perfect scenario for the two of you.

Remember, presenting a diamond engagement ring is optional. While 70 percent of American guys who propose do so by presenting a ring, this is certainly not a requirement or tradition you must adhere to. The engagement ring is merely a symbol of love.

Chinese Fortune Cookie Proposal

Proposal Concept: After a Chinese dinner, present your girlfriend with a special fortune cookie containing the message, "Will you marry me?"

Approximate Scenario Cost: The customized fortune cookie (less than $10), and the cost of the meal.
*Plus the cost of the engagement ring, if used.

Approximate Preparation Time: Minimal (overnight shipping of the fortune cookie is available for a fee).

Supplies/Equipment Needed: Customized Fortune Cookie.

Location: At a Chinese restaurant or at home (using take-out).

Related Contact Information/ Resources:

Fortune Cookie Supply Company
818-905-8180
www.fortunecookiesupply.com

Victory Store
http://store.yahoo.com/victorystore00/ilforcook.html

For many dating couples, a Chinese food dinner, eaten either in the restaurant or as takeout, is a popular dining option when nobody wants to cook. If Chinese food dinners are a somewhat regular part of your life, consider using this as the stage to pop the question. After dinner, when the waiter presents you with your fortune cookies, make sure the cookie your girlfriend receives is a special one—one that contains the message, "Will you marry me?"

Once she opens the fortune cookie, get down on one knee, present an engagement ring, and formally ask for her hand in marriage. Fortune cookies with customized messages within them can be ordered from the companies listed on page 79. Some Chinese restaurants may also keep these special cookies in stock, so it's a good idea to speak with the restaurant's manager in advance. Assuming your proposal is accepted, have the waiter ready to deliver exotic drinks to the table for a special toast.

A similar scenario can be created at home, if you order Chinese takeout. You can swap the regular fortune cookies provided with a cookie containing your special message, then have a bottle of champagne chilled and ready to pour for a special toast. By proposing at home, you'll have privacy. You can also create a romantic setting by adding candlelight and music that has special meaning to you both (such as the first song to which you ever danced together).

Live Butterfly Release Proposal

Proposal Concept: Your girlfriend opens a basket and dozens of live, colorful butterflies fly out and surround you both. At the bottom of the basket is the engagement ring and a note asking, "Will you marry me?" which she reads, as the butterflies fly around.

Approximate Scenario Cost: $75 to $100 per dozen butterflies, plus the cost of the basket. Depending on the size of the basket, between one and three dozen butterflies will make a wonderful presentation.

*Plus the cost of the engagement ring.

Approximate Preparation Time: Order the butterflies at least one week in advance. Be prepared to propose within 24 hours after receiving the living butterflies.

Supplies/Equipment Needed: A minimum of one dozen live butterflies, a basket (with a cover), an engagement ring and your personalized "Will you marry me?" note.

Location: You'll want to execute this idea outdoors, in warm weather.

Related Contact Information/Resources:

The Butterfly Collection
800-548-3284
www.Bufferflycelebration.com

Butterfly & Nature Gift Store
888-395-7324
www.butterfly-gifts.com/livebutterflyreleases.html

Amazing Butterflies
800-808-6276
www.amazingbutterflies.com/basket.htm

Plan a romantic picnic, walk along the beach, nature hike, or some other intimate, outdoor activity with your girlfriend. When you're ready to propose, present her with the basket that's covered with a screen-like mesh cloth. Upon opening the basket, at least one dozen large and colorful live butterflies fly out and surround you both. (Don't worry, they're totally harmless.) At the bottom of the basket will be your personalized note with the message, "Will you marry me?" and the sparking engagement ring.

This can help you create an extremely unique, romantic, and memorable moment. Most suppliers of living butterflies request that you place your order at least seven to 10 days prior to when you plan to propose, then arrange to have the butterflies shipped via overnight courier to ensure their safe arrival. For this concept to work (and for the safety of the butterflies), the outdoor temperature should be at least 62 degrees when the butterflies are released. You should also plan to release the butterflies at least 30 minutes before sunset.

Amazing Butterflies ships butterflies that are USDA approved for your area of the country, so you will only receive butterflies indigenous to your area. According to the company, if there are flowers and host plants for the butterflies nearby, they may stay a while or even take up residency for the remainder of the season. When you're preparing the special basket from which the butterflies will be released, Amazing Butterflies suggests transferring the butterflies to your basket before transporting them to where the proposal will take place. Complete care, handling, and release instructions for your butterflies will be sent along with the order.

To create the ideal butterfly release basket, you can pay a company, such as Amazing Butterflies, to do the work for you, or you can use your own creativity and follow these steps, adapted from those suggested by Amazing Butterflies:

Making Your Own Butterfly Release Basket

1. Purchase a nice wicker basket from any craft store. A basket should cost no more than a few dollars.

2. Drape tulle (veil material) over the basket to keep the butterflies from escaping and to create a screened-in enclosure.

3. Create a card or note that says, "Will you marry me?" This can be a traditional greeting card or something more original that you create using calligraphy, glitter, or other arts and crafts materials. Place the card, along with a jewelry box containing the engagement ring, at the bottom of the basket (but fully visible once it's opened).

4. Once the basket is prepared and your "Will you marry me?" message and the ring are placed and secured inside (using tape, for example) transfer the butterflies into your release basket. Remove the butterflies from the envelopes in which they arrive and place them in the basket.

5. When all the butterflies are safely in the basket, using a colorful ribbon, tie the veil material closed. Remember, you want to transfer the butterflies to the basket before you get to the location where you'll be proposing. Until you are ready to pop the question, keep the basket covered using a towel to shield the butterflies from light until arriving at the location.

6. To ensure the butterflies will be awake and active, warm them up prior to their release by exposing by exposing them to light.

7. When you're ready to propose, present the basket to your girlfriend and have her untie the netting material to release the butterflies and expose your "Will you marry me?" message and engagement ring.

Christmas Proposal

Proposal Concept: During a Christmas Eve or Christmas Day family gathering, present the ultimate gift to your girlfriend—an engagement ring.

Approximate Scenario Cost: Free, except for the cost of an optional Santa Claus suit rental. (The costume rental or purchase should cost between $100 and $200.)
    *Plus the cost of the engagement ring.

Approximate Preparation Time: Less than one week.

Supplies/Equipment Needed: Engagement ring and/or Santa Claus suit.

Location: Anywhere.

Related Contact Information/Resources:

Local costume supply shop (consult the phone book).

Planet Santa (Pierre's Costumes)
215-925-7121
http://store.planetsanta.com
www.costumers.com

Costume World
800-423-7496
www.costumeworld.com/xmas.html

Christmas is one of the most popular times of the year to propose marriage. You can propose when you and your significant other are alone and standing in front of the Christmas tree, for example. You might, however, choose to pop the question in front of the entire family (during Christmas Eve dinner or on Christmas Day, when everyone is opening their gifts).

There are obviously many different approaches you can take to actually popping the question. For example, you can simply gift wrap the engagement ring and present it to her as one of her holiday gifts (placing it under the tree). Then when she opens it, you can drop to one knee and propose formally. To create an added element of surprise, you can gift-wrap the ring in a small box, wrapped within a medium-size box, that's wrapped within a larger box. Thus, your girlfriend will initially think the gift (containing the ring) is just another present, such as a sweater, for example. Only after she opens several of the boxes within boxes will the ring be revealed.

Depending on the type of person you are, you can also dress up in a Santa Claus costume (which you rent from a local costume shop), then as Santa, present her with your engagement ring while getting down on one knee.

As with any proposal idea, you can customize the setting by having a fire blazing in the fireplace, lighting up the Christmas tree with twinkling lights, having special music playing in the background, and by sharing a special toast with a glass of wine or champagne. The objective is to make your girlfriend's holiday season even more festive by giving her your commitment to marry her (and an engagement ring) as a Christmas gift.

[Legal note: In some states, when you present an engagement ring as a Christmas gift (or for any holiday), it is considered a gift that does not necessarily have to be returned if the engagement is later called off.]

New Year's Eve Proposal

Proposal Concept: Ring in the New Year, the night of December 31, by proposing marriage when the clock strikes midnight.

Approximate Scenario Cost: Free, or the cost of admission to whatever New Year's Eve party you choose to attend.
Plus the cost of the engagement ring, if used.

Approximate Preparation Time: Minimal.

Supplies/Equipment Needed: The engagement ring and some champagne.

Location: At home, a New Year's Eve party, or even in New York City's Times Square.

Related Contact Information/Resources: Not Applicable.

At the stroke of midnight, as you ring in the New Year, you propose marriage and kick off the new year by giving up your bachelorhood. Whether you propose at a New Year's Eve party surrounded by friends and family, travel to New York City and propose in the heart of Times Square with Dick Clark and a few hundred thousand of your closest friends, or you plan a romantic evening alone with your girlfriend, you can use the New Year's holiday to reflect on your times together as a dating couple and then make the New Year's resolution to spend the rest of your lives together as husband and wife.

Your New Year's Eve proposal might involve getting down on one knee, proposing after a romantic dinner, or otherwise picking the perfect locale to pop the question right at midnight.

If you plan to travel to New York City and propose at or around midnight, while attending the festivities in Times Square, you might consider contacting the producers of *Dick Clark's New Years' Rockin' Eve*, or any of the other television shows that broadcast live on the other TV networks, like MTV. While it's not common practice for these shows to allow live marriage proposals, exceptions are sometimes made. Thus, you might be able to propose on live, national television. You'll want to contact the various TV producers several weeks in advance. Dick Clark Communications, for example, can be reached at 818-841-3003. MTV's main number is 212-258-8000.

Valentine's Day Proposal

Proposal Concept: Capitalize on this holiday, based on love and romance, to get engaged.

Approximate Scenario Cost: Varies, based on how extravagant you make the event.
Plus the cost of the engagement ring.

Approximate Preparation Time: Varies.

Supplies/Equipment Needed: Engagement ring plus (optional) chocolates, roses, rose petals, teddy bear, wine/champagne, etc.

Location: Anywhere.

Related Contact Information/Resources:

Godiva
800-9-GODIVA
www.godiva.com

Build-A-Bear Workshop
877-789-BEAR
www.buildabear.com

Vermont Teddy Bear Company
800-829-BEAR
www.vermontteddybear.com

The Story of Valentine's Day
www.holidays.net/amore/story.html

America Online's Create A Love Poem
AOL Keyword: Valentine Love Poetry
http://aolsvc.virtualpoetry.aol.com//feature/valentines

While some call Valentine's Day (February 14) the ultimate "Hallmark holiday," those who are true romantics at heart use this holiday to annually communicate their love to others, especially those close to them. Thus, with so much romance in the air around mid-February, it makes perfect sense that so many couples get engaged on Valentine's Day.

Following the Valentine's Day theme of love and romance, there are a multitude of things you can do to make your proposal extra special, plus maintain the element of surprise until you actually pop the question. After all, your significant other will expect you to do something romantic on this holiday, so planning a romantic dinner or getaway probably won't raise too much suspicion if you're planning a proposal surprise.

You can combine your marriage proposal on Valentine's Day with one or more extra romantic gestures, such as spreading rose petals around the room in which you plan to propose or presenting a dozen or more long-stemmed roses.

In terms of your actually proposal, you can present your girlfriend with an engagement ring by purchasing a small box of assorted chocolates and hiding the ring among the chocolates. Godiva, for example, offers small boxes of four gourmet truffles packed in a trademark gold box (Truffle Assortment 2.5 ounce, item #73100, $7). You could easily remove one of the truffles and replace it with your engagement ring, then reseal the box. On Valentine's Day, present her with flowers and the small box of chocolates after dinner, for example. Insist that she try one of the truffles for dessert. When she opens the box, be prepared to pop the question when she finds the ring.

Another romantic way to present your engagement ring on Valentine's Day is to purchase a cute teddy bear. Using a string or small gold chain, for example, tie the engagement ring around the teddy bear's neck, like a necklace. Many upscale malls now have a Build-A-Bear Workshop store. You might want to visit one of these stores (or the company's Website) and purchase a teddy bear dressed like a bride. The "I Do Curly" teddy bear (Item #2458/1957, $30) comes dressed in a glamorous bridal gown ensemble. It's even possible to add a "Build-A-Sound" message and create a speaking teddy bear that will pop the question for you.

The Vermont Teddy Bear Company offers its 15-inch Bride Bear (Item #KK0015578, $85.95), which features a beautiful bear dressed like a bride in a lovely satin and tulle wedding gown and veil, complete with bouquet. You can choose from a variety of options to totally customize your teddy bear, making it the perfect accessory to help you pop the question with finesse and style.

Another extremely romantic way of proposing, if you feel like being creative and allowing your true romantic side to shine, is to write a love poem and recite it to your significant other on Valentine's Day. Of course, you can always get your hands on a poetry book and recite some-one else's poem as you prepare to propose. America Online (keyword: Valentine Love Poetry) offers a fun, on-screen tool to help you write your own romantic poem and communicate your sentiments of love. There's also the I Love Poetry Website (*www.ILovePoetry.com*), which is an excellent resource for those looking to pop the question with poetic style.

Vermont Teddy Bear Company's Bride and Groom Bears.

Be a Knight in Shining Armor...Or a Chicken!

Proposal Concept: Show up at your girlfriend's place of work or her home dressed up like a knight in shining armor (or another costume) in order to propose.

Approximate Scenario Cost: $100 to $300 for the costume rental.
Plus the cost of the engagement ring, if used.

Approximate Preparation Time: Less than one week.

Supplies/Equipment Needed: Costume, engagement ring, and flowers (optional).

Location: Anywhere.

Related Contact Information/Resources:

> Local costume rental shop (consult the phone book).
>
> Blacksmith Armor Sculptor
> 519-669-0721
> *www.thakblacksmith.com/html/rentals.html*

Many women have had dreams of being swept off their feet by a knight in shining armor. Even if you aren't a real-life knight, you can still save the day by dressing up like a genuine knight when you pop the question.

Most costume shops offer knight costumes for rent. Dress up, then show up at your girlfriend's job (or anywhere you know she'll be) to propose. The Blacksmith Armor Sculptor, for example, offers several different, genuine steel knight costumes and related accessories. The company's 15th Century Plate Armor, for example, includes everything you need, such as the armet (helmet), breast and back plate (torso armor), cuisses (leg armor), greaves (shin armor), sabatons (shoes), pauldrons (shoulder armor), couter (arm armor), finger gauntlets (gloves), padded arming jacket, battle ax or sword, and tights. Of course, if you want to go all out, you could also rent a horse and gallop up to your girlfriend's home (or place of work), then ride off into the sunset together.

A more humorous twist on this idea could be used if you've been avoiding getting engaged for a while. Instead of dressing up like a brave knight, you could dress up like a giant chicken (symbolic of you being scared to pop the question), and propose dressed up in bright yellow feathers. Use your imagination to come up with other romantic or humorous costume ideas that would be appropriate to your situation.

For Dessert, Your Engagement Ring Is Served

Proposal Concept: Bring your girlfriend to a nice restaurant for dinner. When dessert is served, in the center of her dessert plate is a box containing your engagement ring, delivered to your table by the waiter.

Approximate Scenario Cost: The price of dinner at the restaurant of your choice.
Plus the cost of the engagement ring.

Approximate Preparation Time: Minimal.

Supplies/Equipment Needed: Engagement ring.

Location: A fancy restaurant.

Related Contact Information/Resources: Contact the headwaiter or manager of the restaurant, in advance, to plan your "special" dessert.

On the premise that you're celebrating a special event, such as a birthday, anniversary of your first date, a promotion at work, or some other occasion, invite your girlfriend for dinner at a fancy restaurant. Throughout dinner, hold a normal conversation. When it's time to order dessert, arrange in advance for the waiter to serve a special plate with the engagement ring displayed in the center. If the restaurant specializes in homemade desserts, they might be able to write, "Will you marry me?" on the plate in chocolate or cake icing.

When dessert arrives, get down on one knee and propose. Have a bottle of champagne ready to be served so you can toast your engagement upon her acceptance. As long as you arrange your plans with the restaurant's manager ahead of time, most fine dining establishments will be more than willing to work with you to coordinate the perfect proposal. If there's a piano player performing in the restaurant, arrange to have your girlfriend's favorite song played as dessert is served.

Move Over Harrison Ford! Make Your Proposal the Feature Presentation

Proposal Concept: Take your girlfriend to the movies. As part of the preshow, arrange to have your "Will you marry me?" message and perhaps a photo displayed prominently on the movie screen.

Approximate Scenario Cost: Varies.
*Plus the cost of the engagement ring, if used.

Approximate Preparation Time: Several weeks.

Supplies/Equipment Needed: A custom 35mm slide created by the company that produces the preshow at the movie theater you plan to attend.

Location: Almost any movie theater.

Related Contact Information/Resources:

National Cinema Network
800-SCREEN-1
www.ncninc.com

Screenvision
212-497-0400
www.screenvision.com

Take your girlfriend to the movies, but make your proposal the feature presentation. Purposely arrive about 15 to 20 minutes before the scheduled show time. While watching the movie theater's preshow on the big screen, all of a sudden your giant customized message appears asking your girlfriend for her hand in marriage.

There are several companies across the United States that produce the preshows for movie theaters. One of the largest is National Cinema Network. While the company typically sells advertising to companies looking to reach moviegoers, it will periodically allow someone to use their advertising vehicle to propose marriage for a nominal fee. Because your slide will only be shown in one theater, prior to one movie, you may be required to pay only for the production costs of your slide.

To determine which company produces the preshow for your local movie theater, contact the theater's management or call the contact number for potential advertisers that's provided during the actual movie preshow.

According to National Cinema Network, "We take your message, place it in an entertainment program on the big screen, and display it every 4.5 minutes in front of a captive audience. Combining movie trivia, theatre announcements, and advertising slides, this entertaining program showcases full-color advertisements on 20-by-40-foot movie screens."

National Cinema Network currently represents more than 10,000 screens in North America, including many theatres in top markets. Screenvision, a competitor, has exclusive access to 13,500 screens, including Loews Cineplex, Carmike Cinemas, and Cinemark.

If you're planning on using this method to propose, contact the preshow producers at least one month in advance, allowing ample time to have the necessary slide(s) produced and provided to the appropriate theater on the night you plan to propose.

An alternative to contacting the preshow producer is to speak directly with your local theater's management. Often they'll be more than willing to help you execute a marriage proposal within their theaters.

One advantage to this proposal idea is that you can invite dozens of your friend and family to attend the movie and see your preshow proposal. Whether or not you actually stay for the movie is entirely up to you.

A slightly more elaborate and expensive spin on this idea is to produce a video featuring you proposing to your girlfriend that would be shown as one of the previews prior to the actual movie. Not all movie theaters are equipped to show video, so you'd have to speak with the theater's management in advance to work out the technical details.

Write "Will You Marry Me?" in the Sand on a Secluded Beach

Proposal Concept: You and your girlfriend take a romantic walk at sunset along a secluded beach. You send her back to the car for something (or somehow distract her), then, while she's not looking, you use a stick to write, "Will you marry me?" in giant letters in the sand.

Approximate Scenario Cost: Free.

> *Plus the cost of the engagement ring, if used.*

Approximate Preparation Time: Minimal.

Supplies/Equipment Needed: A stick to write your message in the sand, and, of course, a sandy beach.

Location: Any beach.

Related Contact Information/Resources: Not Applicable.

Imagine walking along a secluded beach and having your significant other notice a personalized message written in the sand that says, "[insert name], will you marry me? Love, [insert your name]." You then get down on one knee to present her with an engagement ring. After she accepts, you could cuddle on the beach as the sun goes down.

Depending on how secluded the beach actually is, you may be able to write the message in the sand, in advance, and hide a bottle of champagne and glasses nearby, then have a friend (or someone from the beachfront resort, if you're staying at one) stand guard while you bring your girlfriend to this special spot on the beach to propose.

As you're walking along the beach, you can start discussing how much your girlfriend means to you, how special your time together has been, and reminisce about happy times you've spent together. This would lead up to your proposal.

Create a Scrapbook of Your Relationship

Proposal Concept: Create a photo album/scrapbook depicting highlights of your relationship thus far. On the last page of the scrapbook, present a "Will you marry me?" message along with a blank space for a photo of the marriage proposal you're about to enact.

Approximate Scenario Cost: Less than $100.
Plus the cost of the engagement ring, if used.

Approximate Preparation Time: Varies.

Supplies/Equipment Needed: Photo album or scrapbook, photos and mementos from your relationship, plus a camera to photograph your proposal.

Location: Any.

Related Contact Information/Resources:

Exposures
800-222-4947
www.exposuresonline.com

Brookstone
866-576-7337
www.Brookstone.com

Sharper Image
800-344-4444
www.SharperImage.com

If you've known your girlfriend for a while, chances are, you, your family, and your friends have a collection of photos from times the two of you have spent together. With the help of your girlfriend's family (who can probably supply additional photos), put together a scrapbook or photo album commemorating and chronicling your relationship thus far.

Include items and mementos from the important times you've spent together. For example, you could incorporate a matchbook from the restaurant where you went for your first date (or a photo of that restaurant), an ad or photo from the first movie you ever saw together and/or something commemorating other fun or romantic times you've spent with each other.

On the final page of the scrapbook or photo album, somehow incorporate a "Will you marry me?" message, perhaps with a photo of the engagement ring you plan to present to her. As you present the ring, have someone take a Polaroid photo of the moment, so you can immediately add this latest event into the scrapbook or album.

When you present the album, ensure the atmosphere and location is perfect for popping the question. Remember, ambiance is important. Add romantic music, candlelight, and so on.

Most Hallmark or arts and crafts stores have an extensive selection of scrapbook products as well as photo albums. The Exposures mail order catalog offers higher-priced and fancy albums and scrapbooks. There are also professional scrapbookers you can hire to put the scrapbook together for you. All you need to do is supply the photos and mementos. To find a professional scrapbooker to hire, ask for a referral at your local craft supply store or use any Internet search engine. Keep in mind, however, the purpose is to create a photo album or scrapbook that showcases your love for your significant other. The album will have a lot more sentimental value if you create it yourself, even if the final product doesn't look totally professional.

Several companies, including Brookstone and The Sharper Image, sell talking picture frames and photo albums. These frames allow you to insert your favorite photo, plus record a short message that can be heard every time a button on the frame is pressed. You could easily propose by taking your favorite picture of you and your girlfriend, placing it in a talking picture frame, recording your proposal message, then presenting your girlfriend with this special gift. At first, she'll think it's just a small token of your love and won't expect the proposal, that is, until she hears the message you recorded.

For $40, Brookstone offers a Leather Picture Frame (item #334631), which records and plays back up to 20 seconds of talking, music, or any other sounds, and holds one 5 x 7, 3 x 5, or 4 x 6 photo. The company also offers a Voice Recording Photo Collage Frame (item # 311738, $45). This frame accommodates five photos and a 10-second recorded message.

Finally, you can create a small photo album chronicling your relationship together, plus add short audio commentary and, ultimately, your proposal message with Brookstone's Talking Photo Album (item #334649, $50). This 20-page album allows you to tell a story using a customized combination of photos, sounds, and words (recorded in your own voice). You can accompany each page of the album with a nine-second recording. The final page of the album can contain your audio marriage proposal along with a photo of you two together. The Sharper Image offers a similar talking photo album (item #GC600, $29.95) that holds 24 pictures (4 x 6) and allows you to record 24 10-second messages.

Scavenger Hunt Leading to the Ring

Proposal Concept: Starting first thing in the morning, provide your girlfriend with a series of clues. Each clue should lead to a small gift and/or another clue. At the end of the day, the ultimate clue leads her to finding an engagement ring and your proposal.

Approximate Scenario Cost: Varies, depending on the number and value of your gifts.
Plus the cost of the engagement ring.

Approximate Preparation Time: Varies.

Supplies/Equipment Needed: Small gifts for your girlfriend to find throughout the day.

Location: Any.

Related Contact Information/Resources: Not Applicable.

Pulling off this type of marriage proposal requires a bit of creativity and planning on your part. It involves creating a series of clues that will lead your girlfriend to finding small gifts and additional clues throughout the day. These could be gifts somehow related to your marriage proposal or totally unrelated, depending on the element of surprise you're trying to create. Each clue can be a riddle or directions leading her to a specific location where she'll pick up the next clue/gift.

Starting in the morning, for example, present your girlfriend with an envelope containing her first clue. Perhaps it could lead her to the restaurant where you and she had your first date. When she gets there, have a gift certificate for a lunch or dinner for two waiting for her to pick up, along with the next clue. The next clue might involve sending her to the dry cleaners to pick up or drop off your tuxedo or one of her dresses. This could hint to her that there's a formal occasion coming up in her future. When she gets there, perhaps a small sentimental gift could be waiting, along with her next clue. Another clue might involve sending her to a local florist. A dozen red roses and her next clue can be waiting for her. You can also use clues that lead her to places where you enjoy spending time together.

Try to incorporate sentimentality, humor, and as much creativity as you can muster into presenting each clue and small gift throughout the day. At the end of the day, the final clue should lead her to the pocket of the jacket you're wearing, where a small box containing an engagement ring will be waiting for her. Of course, you'll need to solicit the cooperation of a handful of people at each location to which you send your girlfriend, so they'll know to present her with your gift and her next clue, without revealing the true reason for the scavenger hunt. Another way to take suspicion away from your true intentions is to present her with a totally unrelated piece of jewelry as one of her gifts, such as a pair of earrings, a necklace, or a bracelet. If she receives jewelry as a gift, for example, she'll think that was the reason for the scavenger hunt and won't suspect the pending marriage proposal. If you present her with additional jewelry, make sure it matches or coordinates well with the engagement ring.

Another way to keep your girlfriend from becoming too suspicious is to use this scavenger hunt proposal idea in conjunction with her birthday, an anniversary of your dating relationship, or some other special occasion. Initially, it'll cause her to think that's the reason for this romantic and fun gesture. At the end of the day, when she finds her final clue, present the engagement ring and pop the question.

Birthday Engagement

Proposal Concept: Present your significant other with a birthday cake. In the center of the cake, surrounded by candles, will be a box with your engagement ring. The message on the cake could say, "Happy Birthday [insert name]. Will you marry me?"

Approximate Scenario Cost: The cost of a custom-decorated cake.
Plus the cost of the engagement ring.

Approximate Preparation Time: One week (to preorder the cake from a bakery).

Supplies/Equipment Needed: Birthday cake, engagement ring.

Location: Any.

Related Contact Information/Resources:

Local bakery (consult the phone book).

Cookies By Design
800-945-2665
www.CookiesByDesign.com

For your girlfriend's birthday, you can either plan a romantic dinner with just the two of you in attendance, or plan a party and invite your friends and family. When it's time to present her with a birthday cake, give her a cake with your proposal message inscribed on it.

If you purchase a cake from a local bakery, it will be able to customize not just the message, but the cake itself, so you can place a small box containing the engagement ring in the center of the cake, without the box or the ring itself getting covered with icing. The cake could also accommodate candles and display the message, "Happy Birthday [insert name]. Will you marry me?" When she sees the message on the cake, be prepared to offer a more formal proposal, by dropping down on one knee, for example.

Of course, if you're presenting her with this special birthday cake during a party, make sure someone is on hand with a camera to capture her expression when she reads the message on the cake and sees the ring for the first time. To maintain the element of surprise, you might want to avoid telling the majority of the party guests what your plans are. If done correctly, the birthday party could quickly transform into an impromptu engagement party!

As an alternative to a birthday cake with your special message, you can also order custom-baked cookies in a variety of wedding- or birthday-oriented shapes and designs, plus have your special proposal message written on the cookies in multicolored icing. Cookies By Design is just one company that creates and ships colorful and delicious customized cookies. Prices range from about $30 to $100 for a seven-cookie arrangement.

Use a Giant Banner to Pop the Question

Proposal Concept: When your girlfriend gets home from work, or returns to her job after lunch, she is greeted by a huge banner that says, "[Insert name] will you marry me?"

Approximate Scenario Cost: $100 or more.
  *Plus the cost of the engagement ring, if used.

Approximate Preparation Time: Several days.

Supplies/Equipment Needed: Custom printed banner.

Location: Any.

Related Contact Information/Resources:

Any local sign printing shop (consult the phone book).

Kinko's
800-2-KINKOS
www.kinkos.com

The expression on your girlfriend's face will be priceless when she sees a giant custom-printed banner, featuring the words "[Insert name], will you marry me?" displayed in giant letters. You can hang the banner at home, at her work, at a special event, in a restaurant, or virtually anywhere you want to pop the question. If you're a sports fan, for example, and you'll be attending a sporting event that will be televised, you could bring a banner and show it off from the stands. You might even get on TV!

Because the banner can be printed on vinyl, it'll become a keepsake that she will cherish for years to come as she reflects fondly on the day you proposed. At Kinko's, you can have a vinyl banner created in a matter of hours, available in four sizes (in feet): 3 x 5, 3 x 8, 3 x 10, and 4 x 12.

When designing your banner to be created at Kinko's, you can have up to eight words displayed in any of 18 different colored letters and in any of 15 different fonts. If you want to use a bit more creativity, add graphic images (such as a photo) to your banner and have it digitally printed, in full color.

As opposed to a banner, at Kinko's you can also have posters printed, laminated, and mounted on FomeCore in two different sizes (in inches): 18 x 24 and 36 x 48. To see all of your various options in terms of having banners and/or posters printed, visit your local Kinko's store or contact any local sign printing company.

Sarah, will you marry me? Love, Peter

Sample Banner

Horse-Drawn Carriage

Proposal Concept: While enjoying a romantic evening in a major city (such as New York City, Chicago, or Boston), you arrange for you and your significant other to take a romantic horse-drawn carriage ride (through Central Park in New York City, for example). During the ride, you propose and present her with a ring.

Approximate Scenario Cost: Varies by location and duration of the ride. You'll typically be charged in 30-minute increments.

Plus the cost of the engagement ring.

Approximate Preparation Time: Minimal.

Supplies/Equipment Needed: Reservations with a horse-drawn carriage service.

Location: Most major cities.

Related Contact Information/Resources:

Directories of horse-drawn carriage companies around the world:

www.angelfire.com/biz/DieGelbeRoseCarriage/ worldwide.html

www.bridalday.com/Transportation/more2.php3

www.allweddingcompanies.com/Weddings/ Transportation/Carriages/

Many cities with large parks or tourist areas offer horse-drawn carriage rides. In New York City, for example, you can take a 30- or 60-minute ride through Central Park. This can be an extremely romantic finale to an evening with your girlfriend. At some significant or scenic point during the ride, you propose.

To find a horse-drawn carriage company in your area, check The Yellow Pages, the Websites listed previously, or use an Internet search engine, such as Yahoo, and enter the search phrase "horse drawn carriage [insert the city name]". If you're in the Boston area, for example, Boston Hansom Cabs (781-391-3079, *www.bostonhansomcabs. com*) and Elegant Touch Carriage Company (781-767-5819 or 800-497-4350, *www.eleganttouchcarriage.com*) offer tours or can be hired to accommodate special requests and occasions.

Bedtime Proposal

Proposal Concept: Fancy hotels turn down the guests' beds before bedtime and often leave a mint or chocolate on each guest's pillow. Using this as a model, as your girlfriend gets ready for bed, place the box containing an engagement ring on her pillow.

Approximate Scenario Cost: None (or the cost of hotel accommodations, if you plan to propose away from home).
Plus the cost of the engagement ring.

Approximate Preparation Time: Minimal.

Supplies/Equipment Needed: None.

Location: Bedroom or hotel room.

Related Contact Information/Resources: Not Applicable.

When you're spending the night together, get ready for bed before your girlfriend and prepare the bedroom by placing the box containing the engagement ring on her pillow (opened for her to see). You can accompany this by sprinkling rose petals on top of the bed or placing a single long stem red rose near the ring. Candles and romantic music can complete this highly romantic setting. (If you're using candles to set the mood, be sure to dim the lights. You don't want it too dark, however, or your girlfriend might not notice the ring on her pillow.)

When your girlfriend sees how you've prepared the bedroom and sees the ring, she'll instantly know what's happening, so be prepared to pop the question in whatever manner is appropriate. Have a bottle of chilled champagne or wine (along with glasses) hidden under the bed, so you can toast your engagement, upon her acceptance of your proposal.

Breakfast in Bed Proposal

Proposal Concept: Wake up before your girlfriend and prepare breakfast in bed for her. In addition to presenting bacon and eggs (or the breakfast of your choice), place the ring under a large covered plate in the center of the tray. She'll uncover the plate expecting breakfast, but she'll be proposed to first.

Approximate Scenario Cost: Minimal.
> *Plus the cost of the engagement ring.*

Approximate Preparation Time: Minimal.

Supplies/Equipment Needed: Tray to serve breakfast in bed, breakfast, and an engagement ring. (If you're staying at a hotel, room service will work too.)

Location: Bedroom or hotel.

Related Contact Information/Resources: Not Applicable.

Start the journey toward spending the rest of your lives together by pampering your girlfriend with a romantic breakfast in bed. Prepare the full breakfast while she's asleep. A few minutes before you're ready to serve breakfast wake up your girlfriend and instruct her to stay in bed. It's important that she be fully awake for the proposal that's about to happen.

Bring the tray from the kitchen, but leave the main course behind. Instead, place the ring on a large plate and cover it with a napkin or some type of cover. You can "garnish" the plate by placing rose petals around the ring. To add to the surprise, place a smaller plate containing a bagel or donut next to the covered plate containing the ring, plus add a glass of juice to the tray for authenticity. (Avoid having hot coffee on the tray. You don't want it to accidentally spill and burn her if she suddenly jumps after realizing that she's being proposed to.)

When your girlfriend is fully awake and waiting in anticipation for her breakfast, carry in the tray, while at the same time, telling her how much you love and appreciate her. Place the tray on the bed and wait for her to uncover the main plate (containing the ring). As she discovers the ring, pop the question in whatever manner you feel is appropriate. Of course, you should also have a real breakfast ready to serve, but chances are, she'll be too excited to eat for a while.

If you'd like to add to this scenario, you can dress up in a tuxedo to serve breakfast and/or present her with a dozen long-stem roses, as you actually propose.

Marry Me Jigsaw Puzzle

Proposal Concept: If your girlfriend enjoys putting together puzzles, have a custom jigsaw puzzle created containing a picture of you both, with the message "Will you marry me?" displayed across the picture.

Approximate Scenario Cost: $17.95 or more.
Plus the cost of the engagement ring, if used.

Approximate Preparation Time: Approximately two weeks to order the custom-printed jigsaw puzzle and have it delivered.

Supplies/Equipment Needed: Photo of you and your girlfriend together. You can scan the photo into your computer and add your message (or have the puzzle creator do this for you).

Location: Anywhere.

Related Contact Information/Resources:

America Online "You've Got Pictures"
AOL Keyword: Pictures. (Select the "Print Store" option)

Custom Puzzle Craft
619-865-7774
www.custompuzzlecraft.com

MGC Custom Made Puzzles
888-604-7654
www.mgcpuzzles.com

Select a favorite photograph of you and your girl-friend together. Scan the image into your computer. Using some type of graphics program, add a text message that says, "[Insert name], will you marry me?" or whatever proposal message you feel is appropriate, to the photo. Next, send the graphic image to a company that will create a custom-designed jigsaw puzzle from your photo.

America Online's "You've Got Pictures" service allows you to take your electronic image, upload it while connected to AOL, add your text message, and then order a cardboard, 7.25 x 11-inch jigsaw puzzle which will be sent directly to your door within a week.

Two companies that will transform your photos into custom designed, handcrafted, wooden jigsaw puzzles are Custom Puzzle Craft and MGC Custom Made Puzzles. Contact each of these companies directly to discuss the many options available, plus visit their Websites to see samples of their work.

According to puzzle crafter John Stokes III, the owner of Custom Puzzle Craft:

> *A Custom Puzzle Craft personal puzzle is a wooden jigsaw puzzle I make for you using a picture or print you provide. I have made quite a few marriage proposal jigsaw puzzles, and you can be assured that I will give your puzzle great personal attention to make your proposal a day you'll always remember fondly. Your puzzle will be a treasure you and yours will want to keep for generations.*
>
> *For marriage proposal puzzles, I can scan your photo or use your digital file to add proposal text as desired. When making your puzzle, I take care to cut it elegantly, and to include the*

proposal text in one or a few "proposal pieces," as needed, in a nice area of the picture. Normally, these proposal pieces are kept by you when presenting the puzzle to your girlfriend, and then 'found' by you and given to your girlfriend after the rest of the puzzle is complete. I am an experienced puzzle maker. If I see anything in your picture or design that I feel needs to be changed, I'll be sure to contact you with a suggestion before starting your puzzle.

How many pieces are good for a proposal? The average count is around 80 pieces, but I've made a few proposal puzzles with more than 200 pieces. Puzzles with 35 to 45 pieces have been popular, as normally you want your girlfriend to complete the puzzle reasonably fast, within 15 minutes.

Puzzles from Custom Puzzle Craft come in a wide range of rectangular and square sizes, ranging from 12 x 10 inches (approximately 30 puzzle pieces) to 25 x 20 inches (approximately 200 puzzle pieces). "Typical sizes for a Marriage Proposal puzzle are 9 x 6 or 10 x 8, with double size pieces," added Stokes.

MGC Custom Made Puzzles also offers specially designed jigsaw puzzles that can be used as tools for helping you pop the question. The company's beautiful, handcrafted, wooden jigsaw puzzles are made to order and cater to the actual individual for whom your puzzle is intended. The "Traditional Cut" wooden puzzles range in size from 5 x 7 inches (between 12 and 70 puzzle pieces) up to as large as 21 x 34 inches (approximately 1,800 puzzle pieces).

Once you have the puzzle created, package it in a fancy gift box and wrap it nicely. Present it as a gift to your girlfriend at a time when you know you and she will be able to spend some quality time together, assembling the puzzle. Have the engagement ring hidden in your pocket until she discovers the true intent of the puzzle and sees the pieces together which spell out your proposal message. At that point, present your ring and pop the question.

A sample marriage proposal puzzle and close-up of the proposal piece from Custom Puzzle Craft.

Write and Recite a Love Poem

Proposal Concept: While down on one knee, for example, recite a love poem to your girlfriend as a prelude to proposing. You could also serenade her with a poem, standing outside her bedroom window.

Approximate Scenario Cost: None.
   Plus the cost of the engagement ring, if used.

Approximate Preparation Time: The time it takes to write and/or practice reciting your poem.

Supplies/Equipment Needed: A love poem.

Location: Any.

Related Contact Information/Resources:

   www.ILovePoetry.com (This is an excellent resource about writing and reciting poetry.)

Whether you choose to be creative and write your own love poem or borrow one from a poetry book, use this as an opportunity to share romantic sentiments that come directly from your heart. Choose a romantic time and location to share your poem, using it as a prelude to popping the question. This can be done after dinner at a romantic restaurant, while you're alone together at home, or your proposal might involve you standing outside her bedroom window and serenading her.

If you're comfortable singing, you could also write and/or perform a song that communicates your love and commitment to your girlfriend. Whether you choose to recite a poem or sing, how you communicate these sentiments should be extremely romantic. What's equally important, however, is what you actually say and why. Choose a poem or song that has a deep, personal meaning to you both and that communicates exactly how you feel about your girlfriend.

If you've written an original poem that you plan to recite, you might want to hire a calligrapher to write out the poem on nice paper and frame it. You can then present a framed copy of the poem to your girlfriend along with the engagement ring. Many places that sell customized wedding invitations, for example, will be able to help you find a calligrapher to transform your poem into a work of art that's suitable for framing. You can also use any Internet search engine and use the search phrase "calligrapher" to obtain a referral.

Propose at the Location Where You First Met

Proposal Concept: Do you remember where and when you first laid eyes on your girlfriend? Where you first met? Where you went for your first date? As you're planning your proposal, consider making one of these locations the place where you pop the question.

Approximate Scenario Cost: Minimal.

*Plus the cost of the engagement ring, if used.

Approximate Preparation Time: Minimal.

Supplies/Equipment Needed: None.

Location: Where you first met or had your first date.

Related Contact Information/Resources: Not Applicable.

When you're ready to propose and you're looking for the perfect spot to pop the question, consider returning to the exact location where the relationship began. Bring your girlfriend to the location where you first met, or someplace you visited on your first date (such as a restaurant), and use this as the location where you propose. Doing this will add a sense of nostalgia to your proposal as you relive the moment you first met and look toward spending the rest of your lives together as husband and wife.

Use the location where you first met as the backdrop for your proposal. Try to recapture as much as possible about that day or night. What were you wearing? What music was playing in the background? What were you doing when you first saw your girlfriend or were introduced to her?

As you recapture the moment you first met, talk about how much your life has changed for the better since that day and how much you look forward to spending many more days, months, and years together. This will set the stage for a romantic proposal. You can then drop to one knee and present an engagement ring.

"Help Wanted: New Bride" Newspaper Ad

Proposal Concept: If you know your girlfriend reads the newspaper regularly, arrange to have an ad containing your proposal printed in the newspaper she reads.

Approximate Scenario Cost: Varies, based on the newspaper and the size of your ad.
Plus the cost of the engagement ring, if used.

Approximate Preparation Time: At least one or two weeks. Contact the newspaper's advertising department for details.

Supplies/Equipment Needed: You need to write the text and plan the ad. (The newspaper will most likely design the ad for you.)

Location: Any.

Related Contact Information/Resources:

Contact the advertising department of your local newspaper. To find your local newspaper, use the Website *www.newspaperlinks.com/home.cfm*.

Your girlfriend will be surprised when she's flipping through the newspaper and spots the ad you plan to use to help you pop the question. Based on the newspaper in which you plan to advertise, you might consider a display ad in the section of the newspaper you know your girlfriend goes to first. Otherwise, you can purchase a classified ad and circle it with a red marker (to ensure that she sees your ad) before your girlfriend gets her hands on the newspaper.

A classified ad in the "Happy Announcements" section of the Sunday *New York Times* national edition (with a 1.7 million circulation), for example, is priced at $31.25 per line, with a four-line minimum. Each line length is between 30 and 35 characters long. You must place your ad by 7 p.m. on the Thursday before the Sunday you wish the ad to run. To place your proposal classified ad in *The New York Times*, call 212-354-3900 or direct your Web browser to *http://nytadvertising.nytimes.com*.

Based on your budget, you might want to incorporate a photo of you and your girlfriend into the ad, along with your text message. This would be considered a *display* ad as opposed to a *classified* ad, and will cost more. The newspaper's advertising department will help you lay-out and design your ad, but you should create the text message yourself to be certain that it's personalized and romantic.

Propose on Live Radio

Proposal Concept: You call up a local radio station, request a song ,and dedicate it to your girlfriend. At the same time, you pop the question on the air.

Approximate Scenario Cost: None.
Plus the cost of the engagement ring, if used.

Approximate Preparation Time: Minimal.

Supplies/Equipment Needed: Radio and telephone.

Location: Any.

Related Contact Information/Resources:

> Contact the request line of your favorite radio station or call the radio station in advance and speak with a producer to coordinate your plan.

While you can probably call your local radio station and request a song anytime, to ensure you'll get your proposal on the air and be able to say exactly what you want to (and when you want to), it's an excellent idea to call the main number (not the request line) of your favorite radio station during normal business hours and talk with the producer of the show on which you want to propose. Coordinate exactly what time your proposal will air, what song you'll request and what you plan to say in advance. Most local radio stations will be thrilled to help you put your proposal on the air. Once the plans for your on-air proposal are set, make sure your girlfriend will be listening to the radio—on the right station and at the right time.

There are a handful of national radio shows that accept requests and would welcome callers to propose on the air. *Open House Party With John Garabedian* is syndicated nationally every Saturday and Sunday night on hundreds of radio stations. Check out the show's Website at *www.OpenHouseParty.com* and call the toll-free request line at 800-669-1010 during the show.

*Other national radio shows
you might want to contact:*

- **American Top 40 with Casey Kasem**
  818-295-5800
  Radio Express
  1415 West Magnolia Blvd.
  Burbank, CA 91506

- **Hollywood Hamilton's Weekend Top 30**
  866-HHT-TOP30, *www.weekendtop30.com*
  1158 26th St., Box 440
  Santa Monica, CA 90403-4698

- **Rick Dees The Weekly Top 40**
  818-845-1027, *www.rick.com*
  KIIS-FM
  3400 Riverside Dr., Suite 800
  Burbank, CA 91505

Modify Your Girlfriend's Computer Screen Saver

Proposal Concept: Modify the screen saver on your girlfriend's computer to flash a "Will you marry me?" message.

Approximate Scenario Cost: None.
  *Plus the cost of the engagement ring, if used.

Approximate Preparation Time: A few minutes.

Supplies/Equipment Needed: Computer (and special screensaver program, if you choose).

Location: Any.

Related Contact Information/Resources: Not Applicable.

If your girlfriend spends a lot of time in front of her computer, when she's not looking, replace her current screen saver with either a simple text message that says, "[Insert Name], will you marry me? Love, [Insert Your Name]," or load a more elaborate screen saver program onto her computer to help with your proposal.

First, get your girlfriend away from her computer long enough to modify the screen saver. Access the properties menu where the screen saver settings are located. (This will vary, depending on the type of computer and the operating system.) Select a screen saver option that displays text. There are often several choices, including 3-dimensional, scrolling, or stationary text. Type your text message in the appropriate area and adjust the font, motion, resolution, and style as you see fit. Adjust the wait time, setting it to the shortest amount of time possible (one minute). This is the amount of time the computer needs to be inactive before the screen saver automatically appears. Once everything is set, distract your girlfriend while she's working on the computer long enough for the screen saver to kick in.

If you're somewhat computer savvy, instead of using a text screen saver, you can create a series of customized photos and graphics and use a picture screen saver. With this option, you can display a series of photos showcasing the history of your relationship and finish off with a customized photo and special text message. You'll need to use a graphics/photo manipulation program to modify your photo(s) once they're in electronic format.

You can also download special screen saver creation programs that allow you to quickly and easily create flashy screen savers with little computer expertise. Combine photos with sound and music in order to create the perfect high-tech marriage proposal. Here are details about just a few screen saver creation programs for PCs:

- Screen Paver—$12.95, *www.screenpaver.com*.

- ScreenTime Media, Photo & Video: Personal Edition—$19.95, *www.screentime.com*.

- Screen Saver Maker—$15 to $40, *www.screen-saver-maker.com*.

This proposal concept will work best if you're in the same room as your significant other when the screen saver kicks in and displays your proposal message. Once your girlfriend sees your proposal message on her computer screen, be prepared to present the engagement ring and ask her to marry you in person. This idea is a great way to surprise her with a marriage proposal while she's working, surfing the Web, writing e-mails, or doing almost anything else on her computer.

Creating a customized screen saver that your girlfriend will see while you're standing next to her in the room is very different from popping the question via e-mail or an Instant Messaging program, for example, which isn't at all romantic and is extremely impersonal.

Commemorate the Occasion by Naming a Star

Proposal Concept: Have a star named after your girlfriend and, at the same time, commemorate the date of your engagement.

Approximate Scenario Cost: $48 to $149.

*Plus the cost of the engagement ring, if used.

Approximate Preparation Time: Two to nine business days.

Supplies/Equipment Needed: Star registry package.

Location: Any.

Related Contact Information/Resources:

International Star Registry
800-282-3333
www.starregistry.com

Star Foundation
888-877-STAR
www.BuyAStar.net

Okay, this idea may sound a little hokey, but if done correctly, it can be a romantic way to help you propose. Through the companies International Star Registry and Star Foundation, you can name a star after your girlfriend and commemorate the date of your engagement at the same time.

International Star Registry has been around since 1979. When you place an order to name a star, you will receive a gift package that includes a 12 x 16-inch parchment certificate (available framed or unframed) listing the star name of your choice, dedication date, and telescopic coordinates of a specific star. You'll also receive an informative booklet with charts of the constellations, plus a more detailed chart with the star you named circled in red.

According to International Star Registry, "Because these star names are copyrighted with their telescopic coordinates in the book, *Your Place in the Cosmos,* future generations may identify the star name in the directory and, using a telescope, locate the actual star in the sky."

To commemorate the date of your engagement, you'll need to know in advance the exact date you plan to get engaged if you want to present your girlfriend with her International Star Registry certificate when you actually pop the question. You can name the star just after your girlfriend or name it using your soon-to-be family name (such as Jane and Jack Smith). Star names are limited to 35 characters.

Along with the package you order, you'll receive a personalized gift card. You can use this gift card to pop the question, or use the custom-named star as a representation of how your love for your girlfriend transcends the Earth. Like the engagement ring itself, this can be a symbol of your timeless love and commitment.

International Star Registry offers three different star-naming packages (as described on *www.starregistry.com*), including:

The Custom Unframed Package ($54)

- A 12 x 16-inch full color parchment certificate personalized with the star name, date, and co-ordinates.

- A personalized 12 x 16-inch sky chart containing the star name, star date, the constellation, and the location circled in red where your star is in the sky.

- A booklet on astronomy written by a professional astronomer with additional sky charts.

- A letter of congratulations/memorial for the recipient.

The Deluxe Framed Package ($97)

- ❧ A fully framed, 12 x 16-inch full-color parchment certificate personalized with the star name, date, and coordinates. The frame measures 16 x 20 inches and was designed specifically for the gift package. The certificate comes double matted in a gold metallic frame. The accompanying star chart is not framed.

- ❧ A personalized 12 x 16-inch sky chart containing the star name, star date, the constellation, and the location circled in red where your star is in the sky.

- ❧ A booklet on astronomy written by a professional astronomer, with additional sky charts.

- ❧ A letter of congratulations/memorial for the recipient.

- ❧ The package also includes a complimentary personalized wallet card imprinted with the star name and coordinates.

The Ultimate Framed Package ($139)

- ❧ With this package, you'll receive everything from the Deluxe Framed Package, and the personalized star chart is also framed. The second frame measures 16 x 20 inches and matches the frame in the Deluxe package.

Star Foundation also offers several different star-naming packages at different price points. What sets this company apart is that a portion of the proceeds it generates are donated to charity.

Wear Your Proposal Message

Proposal Concept: Have a custom-imprinted T-shirt made that says, "[Insert Name], will you marry me?" and wear it when you pop the question, or place a temporary tattoo somewhere on your body for your significant other to find.

Approximate Scenario Cost: Less than $50.
Plus the cost of the engagement ring, if used.

Approximate Preparation Time: Minimal.

Supplies/Equipment Needed: Custom-imprinted T-shirt or temporary tattoo kit.

Location: Anywhere.

Related Contact Information/Resources:

Body Talk Tattoo Set
Hearts Desire Gift Baskets
866-243-4249
http://heartsdesiregiftbaskets.safeshopper.com

Body Talk Temporary Word Tattoos
866-Send-A-Gift
http://romanceher.com/wordtatoos.htm

Flax Art & Design
888-352-9278
www.flaxart.com

While having a discussion with your girlfriend, you begin taking off your shirt or jacket. Beneath the outer layer of clothing you're wearing is a T-shirt imprinted with the message, "[Insert Name], Will You Marry Me?" As soon as your girlfriend notices the message on the shirt, you formally propose to her.

A more intimate variation of this idea involves placing a temporary text message tattoo somewhere on your body for your girlfriend to find. Depending on how romantic you'd like to get, you can show your girlfriend how sweet you are by purchasing the "Body Talk Tattoo Set" ($14.95). It allows you to imprint your body with the custom text message of your choice using edible chocolate frosting. The kit comes with letter stencils, chocolate body frosting, and applicator. Using this kit, you can create your own message and place it anywhere on your body.

Body Talk Temporary Word Tattoo Kits are also available from companies like 866-Send-A-Gift and Flex Art & Design. The "Romantic" kit ($15), for example, allows you to create a temporary tattoo by mixing and matching upwards of 800 words, symbols, and phrases. You cut out the words, one at a time, then apply them to your skin to create a temporary tattoo with a customized message (in this case, transforming a part of your body into a billboard for your proposal message). The temporary "Will You Marry Me?" or customized message tattoo can later be removed with rubbing alcohol or baby oil.

Customized Crossword Puzzle Proposal

Proposal Concept: Create a custom-designed crossword puzzle for your girlfriend to complete. All of the clues will lead up to the marriage proposal.

Approximate Scenario Cost: Between $40 and $200.
Plus the cost of the engagement ring, if used.

Approximate Preparation Time: One to two weeks.

Supplies/Equipment Needed: Either use crossword puzzle creation software on your computer to create your own puzzle, or hire a professional crossword puzzle creator/writer.

Location: Any.

Related Contact Information/Resources:

Crossword Weaver software (PC-compatible)
800-229-3939
www.crosswordweaver.com

1st Spot Crossword Puzzle Games
http://1st-spot.net/topic_crosswords.html

CustomPuzzles.com
www.custompuzzles.com

Web Games To Go
www.webgamestogo.com

Barbara Johnson (professional crossword puzzle creator)
812-332-3638
E-mail: iambabs@aol.com

Master Puzzlers
E-mail: TP@MasterPuzzles.com
www.masterpuzzles.com

If you and your girlfriend enjoy solving puzzles together and she's a fan of crossword puzzles, consider having a customized crossword puzzle created that will help you pop the question. There are a variety of inexpensive software packages, such as Crossword Weaver ($39.95), that will help you quickly and easily create a professional looking crossword puzzle using all of your own clues or clues created by the software. (Additional online resources are listed in the preceding chart.)

For those of you who aren't too creative, you have the option of hiring a professional crossword puzzle creator, such as Barbara Johnson. Her prices range from $40 to $200, depending on the intricacy of the custom-designed crossword puzzle. The majority of her crossword puzzles are 15-by-15 squares (the size of the daily *New York Times* crossword puzzle) and are priced around $40. A 21 x 21-square puzzle, similar to what appears in the Sunday edition of *The New York Times* will cost approximately $60. Depending on her workload, a puzzle can be created within one week.

Master Puzzles is a leading creator of custom-designed crosswords, trivia contests, puzzles, and assorted games for virtually all media. According to Master Puzzles, they can produce custom-crafted games using your specified subjects or utilizing their vast archive of trivia questions, crosswords, and puzzles to make an instant games section. They have provided hundreds of clients with crossword puzzles, word searches, anagrams, cryptograms, and other games, using only professional, well-published puzzle masters.

Make Your Proposal Magical

Proposal Concept: You don't have to be David Copperfield to amaze your girlfriend by making a diamond engagement ring appear out of nowhere or levitate before her eyes. Surprise her with a touch of magic!

Approximate Scenario Cost: Less than $50.
  *Plus the cost of the engagement ring.

Approximate Preparation Time: One to two weeks.

Supplies/Equipment Needed: Magic trick.

Location: Any.

Related Contact Information/Resources:

Any local magic store (consult the phone book).

Tannen's Magic
212-929-4500
www.tannens.com

Airport Magic Shop
215-492-5171
www.AirportMagicShop.com

MagicTricks.com
www.MagicTricks.com

No matter how you plan to pop the question, you can add a bit of magic to your proposal to make it more exciting. With a little bit of training, practice, and preparation, you can mesmerize and surprise your girlfriend by having a diamond engagement ring appear out of nowhere or levitate before her eyes as you pop the question. To discover how to perform a magic trick involving your engagement ring, visit any local magic shop or call one of the shops listed on page 130. There are a variety of different tricks you can purchase that can incorporate an engagement ring as the primary prop.

Visit any magic store in your area and request that they demonstrate tricks that utilize a "magic box" that can be used to make the engagement ring appear. There are many different tricks available that can help you create this dramatic effect. You show the empty box, say a few magic words, and *presto*, the ring appears within the box.

Using a $30 magic trick called "Float," from Airport Magic Shop, for example, you can make your engagement ring float up out of your hands all around your body, down to the floor, in and out of your pockets, even behind your back, and then float right back to your hands.

The Float trick allows you complete control to make any lightweight object, including an engagement ring, fly all around your body, and even into pockets. The trick comes with an instructional video that will teach you everything in a matter of minutes. It's very easy to learn, yet with a bit of practice will look impressive.

MagicTricks.com offers a trick, called The Quarter Box ($24.95). This trick involves showing your girlfriend a beautiful wooden box that's empty. Say a few magic words, like "I love you!" and an object (the engagement ring) will appear in the box. You can also perform the

Ring Escape trick (available from MagicTricks.com, $29.95). The engagement ring is placed on a bolt, secured there by a nut. A padlock is placed through a hole in the bolt, securing the ring on the assembly. At your command, the ring falls free from the nut and bolt, but the padlock is still locked in place.

Incorporating a "magic act" into your proposal can be fun and entertaining, but to make any magic trick work properly, make sure you practice until your presentation is perfect. Making a ring magically appear or float out of your shirt pocket, for example, is a great way to surprise your girlfriend when you're about to pop the question.

You Have Your Idea. Now What?

Hopefully, one or more of these ideas have started your mind working and you're well on your way to deciding exactly how and when you'll pop the question. In the next chapter, you'll discover another bunch of ideas that can help you create the ultimate memorable moment as you propose marriage to your girlfriend. The ideas you're about to read, however, are a bit extravagant, over-the-top, and less traditional. Some also assume that you have considerable money to spend on your proposal, aside from what you spend on the engagement ring.

Once you have a solid idea in place, make sure you invest the time to carefully plan out all of the details to ensure that your special idea will be executed flawlessly at the right moment. Chapter 5 will help you put together a preproposal checklist to ensure you're well prepared and not forgetting anything important. If all goes well, you should be engaged in no time!

Chapter 3

Extravagant, Outrageous, and Fun Proposal Ideas

specially if you have the money and if investing the time needed to plan an extravagant or over-the-top proposal is within your means, the possibilities for how you can pop the question are truly limitless. This chapter is chock full of ideas that will help you create a marriage proposal scenario that's truly memorable. Just as with any of the ideas offered in the previous chapter, each can be customized to be as romantic or traditional as you'd like, based upon the relationship you have with your significant other.

The marriage proposal ideas offered here will all require a substantial amount of planning on your part, and in many instances, travel is required. If you use travel Websites, however, you'll find some amazing deals that can make even the most extravagant marriage proposal ideas much more affordable.

Thus, if you're planning to whisk your girlfriend away to an exotic locale in order to propose, be sure to shop around for the very best prices on airfare, hotels, rental cars, and other travel accommodations using Websites such as Hotwire.com, Travelocity.com, Priceline.com, Hotels.com, and Orbitz.com.

Whether you'd like to find a secluded location to propose privately or you'd like to become engaged in front of the entire country by popping the question on network television, it's important to focus on what you believe your girlfriend would want in terms of fulfilling her dreams for becoming engaged. As you get caught up in the planning of how you'll propose, it's easy to lose sight of what you're trying to accomplish.

Getting engaged is a time to demonstrate your love and commitment to your girlfriend as you ask her to marry you. However you choose to pop the question, you'll want to ensure you communicate your strong feelings in the most sincere and memorable way possible. Of course, planning something extravagant that's sure to impress her is an option, however, after proper consideration, you may determine that your girlfriend would appreciate a more subtle and traditional proposal. (You can save the extravagance for the wedding or honeymoon.) It's all a matter of understanding your girlfriend's desires and fulfilling them in a way that allows you to demonstrate your love in a memorable way as you ask her to marry you.

Coming up with a unique idea regarding how you'll pop the question can be a challenge. Thus, you'll probably want to take the ideas described in this and the preceding chapter and totally customize them to meet your needs.

At the end of this chapter, you'll read about Korbel Champagne Cellars' annual Perfect Proposal Contest and learn how the company has helped a handful of now married couples create and enact their dream marriage proposal scenarios. Not only will you discover some of the creative ideas the contest's past winners came up with for popping the question, but you'll also discover how Korbel took each winning couple's idea and helped make it a reality. But first, check out these wedding proposal ideas that can best be described as extravagant, outrageous, over-the-top, and fun!

Propose Atop the Eiffel Tower in Paris

Proposal Concept: Pop the question at the top of the Eiffel Tower in Paris, then celebrate at one of the two restaurants in the monument.

Approximate Scenario Cost: The cost of airfare, hotel, etc., plus approximately $15 per person to visit the top of the Eiffel Tower. The cost of dining at one of the restaurants varies, however, Le Jules Verne Restaurant is the more expensive of the two. All together, a three-day trip from the United States to Paris for two could cost anywhere from $800 to $3,000 or more.
Plus the cost of the engagement ring.

Approximate Preparation Time: Several weeks.

Supplies/Equipment Needed: None.

Location: Paris, France.

Related Contact Information/Resources:
    www.tour-eiffel.fr/teiffel/uk/

Altitude 95 Restaurant telephone number for reservations: 33 (0)1 45 55 20 04

Le Jules Verne Restaurant telephone number for reservations: 33 (0)1 45 55 61 44

Paris, France is the city of romance, and when you think about the most romantic place within the city to pop the question, the Eiffel Tower probably comes to mind. Between March 31, 1889 and the end of 2002, more than 204 million people visited the Eiffel Tower.

No matter where you live in the united States, with advanced planning, discounted airline tickets to Paris can be purchased online from a travel-related Website, directly from a major airline, or through a travel agent. Depending on the time of year and various other considerations, a round-trip airfare between a major U.S. city and Paris could be as low as $250 per person. Using one of the discounted travel Websites, a top-notch hotel in Paris can be booked for between $100 and $200 per night.

If you want to maintain the element of surprise, organize a trip to Paris with your girlfriend and spend time planning your itinerary as tourists together. Choose a time to visit the Eiffel Tower. It's open to visitors 365 days a year, usually between 9 a.m. or 9:30 a.m. and 11 p.m. or midnight, depending on the time of year. Once you get to the Eiffel Tower, the lines to take the elevator to the top (the most romantic place to pop the question) might be long, so be prepared for a wait.

Tourists can travel to the first floor (by stairs or elevator), the second floor (by stairs or elevator), or to the top (exclusively by elevator). For current admission prices (which are around $15 per person to visit the top, depending on currency exchange rates), visit the Eiffel Tower Website.

If you're planning to propose atop the Eiffel Tower, consider popping the question around sunset. The view is spectacular. You can then dine and celebrate your engagement at either Altitude 95 or Le Jules Verne Restaurant, both located within the Eiffel Tower. After sunset, the Eiffel Tower is illuminated and is an equally stunning sight.

Le Jules Verne Restaurant is the more formal of the two restaurants in The Eiffel Tower. It is located on the second floor and has its own private elevator access. The head chef, Alain Reix, has brought the restaurant an excellent reputation, placing it among the best in France. Sitting in the heart of this intricate iron structure full of angles and perspectives, the Jules Verne looks out over Paris from 125 meters above ground.

Altitude 95 is located on the first floor. The name comes from its height, which is 95 meters above sea level. The large bay windows of the restaurant look out over the Seine and the Trocadéro to one side and the inside of the Tower to the other. The atmosphere is reminiscent of an airship moored above Paris. The restaurant seats 200 and also has a ground floor bar that serves drinks and refreshments all day. Reservations for either restaurant are definitely recommended.

If you're planning to propose, call the manager of either restaurant in advance. Special seating requests or other arrangements can sometimes be accommodated if made in advance. You can also contact the National Monument Center at 33 (0) 1 44 54 19 30 for additional information. Make sure you bring a camera or video camera to record this very special event.

While popping the question at the top of the Eiffel Tower is extremely romantic and guaranteed to be memorable, there are plenty of national landmarks within the United States that make perfect proposal spots. For example, there's the top of the Empire State Building or the Statue of Liberty in New York City and the top of the Space Needle in Seattle, Washington. In Boston, you can propose and dine at the top of The Prudential Center (at the award-winning restaurant, called The Top of the Hub). There are also places offering natural beauty, such as any of the national parks, the Grand Canyon, or Niagara Falls.

Overseas, there are countless exotic places that make the perfect backdrop for a marriage proposal. The Great Pyramids, The Great Wall of China, Stonehenge, Mount Everest, or any other ancient or modern wonder of the world or landmark might be appropriate.

When choosing a location to propose, consider someplace that's extremely romantic or to which you and/or your significant other have a strong sentimental attachment. For more information about exotic places around the world where you might want to propose, point your Web browser to *http://wonderclub.com/AllWorldWonders.html*.

Pop the Question on Network Television

Proposal Concept: Share your proposal with your girlfriend and potentially millions of TV viewers.

Approximate Scenario Cost: None.
             Plus the cost of the engagement ring, if used.

Approximate Preparation Time: Up to several weeks.

Supplies/Equipment Needed: Proposal sign or banner.

Location: TV studio.

Related Contact Information/Resources:

Contact the producers of the show with which you'd like to coordinate your proposal. Keep in mind, the morning network TV shows originate from New York City. Many of the popular television talk shows are filmed in New York, Chicago, or Los Angeles.

If you have your heart set on proposing on national, network television, one of the easiest ways to do this (although it's not guaranteed to work) is to show up in front of NBC's *The Today Show* studios at Rockefeller Center in New York City during a live broadcast of the popular morning show. Every day, those who attend the show in person and watch the broadcast from outside the studio typically get seen on television. To help ensure your chances of getting TV exposure, create a large and colorful banner that spells out your marriage proposal and be sure to hold it up during the broadcast. Also, try to get the attention of one of the show's producers, camera people, production assistants, or one of the hosts (during a commercial break, for example) and tell them what you'd like to do. At the very least, you should get a chance to have your proposal banner displayed on TV. If time permits, the producers might even let you talk on the air and propose live.

The week of Valentine's Day, many of the television morning shows, as well as the various talk shows, produce romantic-themed segments. Many of these shows actively look for people looking to propose marriage or get married on national television, however, these segments are planned up to two months in advance.

Aside from the network morning shows—*The Today Show* (NBC), *Good Morning America* (ABC), and *The Early Show* (CBS)—all of which broadcast live from New York City, consider contacting producers at popular television talk shows, such as *Oprah, Live! With Regis and Kelly, The Jerry Springer Show, The Caroline Rhea Show, The Other Half, The View, The John Walsh Show, Dr. Phil,* or daytime variety shows, such as those hosted by Ellen DeGeneres, Sharon Osborne, or Ryan Seacrest. See if you can appear as a guest to surprise your girlfriend and propose. These and others shows like them originate from studios in New York City, Chicago, and Los Angeles.

To contact the producers at any TV show, look at the show credits at the end of the broadcast and see what network and at what studio the show is taped or produced from. Next, call information and obtain the phone number for that studio. Call the studio and ask for the production office for the show you'd like to contact. Once you reach the show's production office, explain what you're looking to do and ask to speak with the appropriate producer.

For example, to contact *The Today Show* in New York City, call The NBC Television Network's main number in New York (212-664-444) and ask for *The Today Show's* production office. You can reach The ABC Television Network in New York at 212-456-7777, and CBS at 212-975-4321.

At the time this book was written, Banyan Productions, the company behind such TV shows as The Learning Channel's *Trading Spaces* and *A Wedding Story,* was in preproduction for a new series, called *Perfect Proposal.* This half-hour program was looking for people looking to surprise their girlfriend (or boyfriend) with a marriage proposal. For details about this show, contact the producers at 215-928-2309 or point your browser software to *www.banyanproductions.com.*

Score Big by Proposing at a Major Sporting Event

Proposal Concept: While attending a professional sporting event at an arena or stadium, you can propose by displaying a giant banner (from the stands) or having a special message appear on the animated scoreboard.

Approximate Scenario Cost: Admission to the sporting event plus a donation to the team's charity is typically required.

Plus the cost of the engagement ring, if used.

Approximate Preparation Time: One to two weeks.

Supplies/Equipment Needed: None.

Location: Any major sports arena or stadium.

Related Contact Information/Resources:

Contact the public relations department for the sports team or the person in charge of the team's scoreboard/animated billboard. This person can be found by calling the team's administrative or executive offices.

Are you a major sports fan? More importantly, is your significant other? If you answered yes to *both* questions, you might consider popping the question at a major sporting event, such as a Major League Baseball game. There are several ways you can do this. First, you might be able to coordinate directly with the team, arena, or stadium in order to step onto the field and propose live in front of all the fans. This should be planned several weeks in advance by contacting the sports team's public relations office. Ask for the person in charge of coordinating or producing the pregame, postgame, or half-time show.

Another way to propose at a major sporting event is to prearrange for your proposal message or video to be displayed on the arena's or stadium's animated scoreboard or billboard. This, too, must be coordinated in advance by contacting the person in charge of the scoreboard/billboard. Call the team's administrative or executive offices to determine the right person with whom you need to speak. Before calling, however, have a general idea of what type of message you'd like displayed and know approximately when you'd like to propose. Take a look at the team's home game schedule in advance.

Perhaps the easiest way to propose at a major sporting event is to create a large banner that you and a friend can display from your seats. While not guaranteed to work, you should be able to capture the attention of TV cameras (if the event is televised), or at least get your picture and the banner displayed on the stadium's/arena's animated scoreboard.

During any New York Yankees home game, for example, you can have your proposal message appear on the Yankee Fan Marquee sometime during the game by making a $75 donation to the New York Yankees Foundation (a program that donates funds for educational and recreational programs for youth organizations throughout New York). A maximum of 10 messages are displayed each game and can be reserved on a first-come basis. For details, contact Yankee Stadium at 718-579-4464 or visit the team's official Website (*http://newyork.yankees.mlb.com*), then select "Yankee Stadium" followed by the "Yankee Fan Marquee" option.

Like all professional sports teams, during a Boston Red Sox home game at Fenway Park, the center scoreboard can be used to display your marriage proposal message for a charitable donation of $100 to the Red Sox Foundation. Donations must be received by noon on the day of the game or by the end of the day Friday for weekend games in order for messages to appear. For additional information or for answers to questions regarding the message board policy, call 877-RED-SOX9 or 617-375-0900.

To have your message displayed during any sporting event at any arena or stadium, begin by visiting the team's official Website for details on how to coordinate your message. You should also call the appropriate person at the arena or stadium directly to work out the details of your proposal and confirm the timing. Once your proposal message appears on the scoreboard or animated billboard, chances are, all eyes from the spectators will be on you and your girlfriend. Be ready to present her with an engagement ring and drop to one knee and propose. You'll probably want to have someone on-hand to videotape or at least photograph the event, because thousands of people will most likely cheer once your girlfriend accepts your proposal.

Proposing at a major sporting event is definitely a memorable and fun way to get engaged, but only if both you and your girlfriend are avid sports fans. If your girlfriend isn't into sports, she might not think that being proposed to at a sporting event is too romantic. Remember, when you propose, you need to cater to your girlfriend's dreams, desires, and wishes—as well as your own.

Spell out Your Proposal on the Sky

Proposal Concept: Have your proposal message displayed in the sky.

Approximate Scenario Cost: Approximately $1,000 per message.

Plus the cost of the engagement ring, if used.

Approximate Preparation Time: One to four weeks.

Supplies/Equipment Needed: Clear sky conditions required.

Location: Any.

Related Contact Information/Resources:

East Coast Skytypers: 718-507-5220

West Coast Skytypers: 562-598-8577

South East Skytypers: 954-791-7936

www.SkyTypers.com

Tom King Aerial Enterprises
800-995-KING

National Directory of Aerial Advertising Companies:
www.pilotshack.com/AerialAdvertising.html

Skywriting or "skytyping" is somewhat expensive, but an extremely fun and memorable way to pop the question to your girlfriend, with as many as two million additional spectators. The concept is simple. You hire an airplane pilot to write your message in the sky. Your 30-character (maximum) message will be upwards of 1,200 feet tall and will stretch up to five miles long across the sky.

Skywriting involves one small airplane releasing smoke from its tail as it spells out your message in the sky. The text will look almost like freehand writing. Skytyping on the other hand is easier to read. This system utilizes five airplanes that fly abreast, 250 feet apart, and "type" up to a 30-character message in a dot-matrix-like pattern. According to Skytypers.com, the message can often be seen for 15 miles in any direction.

Based in New York, California, and Florida, Skytypers can create your message in the sky above most major East Coast and West Coast cities. The rates start at $1,000 for each message.

Tom King Aerial Enterprises has a network of planes and pilots across America. This company offers another alternative to skywriting. Small planes tow large banners or aerial billboards across the sky. Smaller skywriting companies are available for hire across America and throughout the world. Check your city's local Yellow Pages for details. For traditional skywriting (or skytyping), your message will stay in the sky for between 10 and 20 minutes, depending on weather conditions.

While the message that appears in the sky will have broad visibility, proper planning and scheduling will be required to ensure that you and your girlfriend are at the best possible viewing spot at the right time. The company you hire will help you choose the best viewing spot and time of day for your message to be displayed.

Keep in mind, clear skies and daylight are needed for skywriting or skytyping to be visible. It's best to keep your proposal message as short as possible in terms of the number of characters and spaces to insure maximum readability. For example, "JULIE_WILL_YOU_MARRY_ME?" would be 24 characters (including spaces) in length.

Get Her Attention with a "Will You Marry Me?" Billboard

Proposal Concept: Rent a giant outdoor billboard located along a major road or near where your girlfriend works to help communicate your proposal message.

Approximate Scenario Cost: Varies.
Plus the cost of the engagement ring, if used.

Approximate Preparation Time: Several weeks.

Supplies/Equipment Needed: None.

Location: Any.

Related Contact Information/Resources:

Ads On Wheels
800-237-6694
www.adsonwheels.com

Electronic Marketing Company
610-353-9300
www.emc-outofhome.com

Outdoor Mobile Media
800-925-8772
www.outdoormobilemedia.com

Outdoor billboards come in a wide range of sizes. They're designed to capture the attention of passersby with large, bold graphics and text, along roadways and in other areas where many viewers will take notice. A typical outdoor billboard is commonly as large as 14 x 48 feet (and often larger).

Imagine your girlfriend's surprise when she's driving to work one morning and spots a billboard with a photograph featuring you and her along with your marriage proposal message. This is a sure way to get hundreds, thousands, or potentially millions of people in your area discussing your proposal as they, too, see the billboard, which might be displayed for a day, week, or month, depending on your budget.

The cost of renting an outdoor billboard varies greatly, based on the size of the billboard, the geographic location, and the duration your message will appear. Typically, the company that owns the outdoor billboards in your area will have its name directly on the billboard, so you can contact the company directly to determine its advertising rates and the cost for producing the artwork to be displayed on the billboard. You can also research outdoor billboard advertising in the Yellow Pages or online using any search engine. To find an outdoor billboard company in your city and state, you can also point your Web browser to *http://business.superpages.com/business/Advertising+ Outdoor+&+Billboard.html.*

If there are no large billboards near where you live, Outdoor Mobile Media, Ads On Wheels, and Electronic Marketing Company each has fleets of large, specially designed trucks that display billboard-size messages on three sides. The message size is 18 x 9 feet on two sides, plus 6 x 9 feet on the back. These trucks can be driven virtually anywhere and customized with your proposal message. The cost isn't cheap, but having a mobile billboard at your disposal for a day will allow you to create a surprise proposal your girlfriend won't soon forget. The cost of a mobile billboard from Outdoor Mobile Media, for example, is based upon where you're located (the company is based in Florida) and how long the billboard truck will be used. There's also an additional $1,500 printing charge to have the truck customized.

Propose in a 15th-Century European Castle

Proposal Concept: If your girlfriend wants a storybook-like proposal, give it to her. Travel to Spain or Portugal, for example, and propose in a real-life, historic castle.

Approximate Scenario Cost: The price of travel, plus accommodations at or near a castle. Staying at a Pousada (hotel) costs between $100 and $300 per night.
*Plus the cost of the engagement ring, if used.

Approximate Preparation Time: Several weeks.

Supplies/Equipment Needed: None.

Location: A European country, such as Spain or Portugal.

Related Contact Information/Resources:

> Pousadas de Portugal
> Reservations and information:
> +351 218 442 001
> Fax: +351 218 442 085
> E-mail: guest@pousadas.pt
> *www.pousadas.pt*

> Portuguese National Tourist Office
> 800-PORTUGAL
> *www.portugal.org*

Storybook-like marriage proposals, compete with a luxury suite in a real-life, 15th-century castle are possible if you hop a plane and travel to Portugal, Spain, or virtually any European country. Portugal, for example, is known for its more than 40 Pousadas, which are three- to five-star hotels that are owned and operated by the Portuguese State. Spain also offers these unique lodging opportunities.

What's unique about these hotels is that some of them, called Historic Pousadas, are fully restored historic buildings, such as castles, former convents, or monasteries. These castles, surrounded by nature, can provide the perfect backdrop for a romantic proposal. While modern facilities, such as electricity, phones, and plumbing have been added to these historic structures, all of the design elements, décor, and even some of the furnishings are authentic.

The majority of the Historic Pousadas are located in remote areas, so, as you leave the city (by car or bus), you'll feel like you're leaving the modern day behind as you travel across miles of beautiful farmland to the remote locations where these castles and monasteries were originally built.

Pousada Castelo de Alvito, for one, is a lovely 15th-century castle in the village of Alvito, Portugal. Its architecture and furnishings reflect the culture of the region. The surrounding gardens, which were once the agricultural land around the medieval castle, make this a very relaxing location. This Pousada has only 20 rooms and is located about 40 kilometers from the city of Evora.

Another of the Historic Pousadas, Monte de Sta. Luzia Pousada, offers spectacular views from each of the 48 rooms and suites, plus it overlooks the city of Viana do Castelo and the sea. Its surrounding gardens and woods, the outdoor swimming pool, and the peaceful place where this Pousada is set, offer a truly romantic and tranquil setting. It's located about 70 kilometers from Oporto. Fishing, golf, tennis, swimming, and nature hiking are among the nearby activities.

Pousada de Estremoz is located within the castle of Estremoz and is the result of the restoration of the magnificent palace that King D. Diniz built for his wife, Queen Santa Isabel. The 31 rooms, two suites, and public areas are chock full of antiques and historical items, while the private palace gardens and modern swimming pool area offer a superb view of the city of Estremoz and the vast Alentejo plain. Located about 110 miles from Lisbon, this is a nice place to stay if you're driving from Portugal toward Spain along the EN4 roadway.

In addition to their authentic beauty, the Pousadas are all relatively small, each offering fewer than 40 guestrooms or suites. Each location also has its own restaurant, where only authentic regional and local cuisine and wines are served. Because the Pousadas are located in remote locations, they're ideal for romantic getaways. If you're looking for activities and sightseeing, however, you might consider spending just one or two nights at one of the Pousadas (where you can propose), then travel to Lisbon (or even Madrid, Spain) to celebrate your engagement.

Roundtrip airfare to Portugal, is offered by TAP Air Portugal, British Airways, American Airlines, and United Airlines, from most major U.S. cities. To learn more about Portugal, visit the Welcome to Portugal Website, Portugal's official tourism site (*www.portugal.org*), or call the Portuguese National Tourist Office at 800-PORTUGAL.

Up, Up, and Away: Pop the Question While Riding in a Hot Air Balloon

Proposal Concept: Charter a hot air balloon and take an early-morning or evening sail through the sky as you pop the question.

Approximate Scenario Cost: Between $340 and $400 (per couple).
Plus the cost of the engagement ring, if used.

Approximate Preparation Time: At least one week advance reservation required.

Supplies/Equipment Needed: None.

Location: A rural area where hot air balloons can be chartered. Good weather is mandatory.

Related Contact Information/Resources:

Soaring Adventures of America
800-762-7464
www.800soaring.com

The United States Hot Air Balloon Team
800-76-FLY-US
www.ushotairballoon.com

1-800-SKY-RIDE.com
800-759-7433
www.1800skyride.com

What could be more romantic than sailing through the air in a hot air balloon and proposing to your significant other as you watch the sun rise? While there are hundreds of hot air balloon charter companies located throughout the world, Soaring Adventures of America, Inc., is the largest network of hot air balloon companies in America, with more than 200 locations. The company has in excess of 24 years' experience and is responsible for well over 300,000 successful hot air balloon rides with a 100-percent safety record.

The Great American Hot Air Balloon Ride (priced at $340 per couple) has room for between one and four passengers per balloon. Your adventure typically begins very early in the morning (an hour or so before sunrise), when the winds are the calmest. The crew chief will escort you and your companion to the hot air balloon's launch site. This is where the balloon gets inflated. Once you're aboard for your ride, the FAA commercially certified pilot will allow the hot air balloon to gently ascend upward and float between 500 and 1,000 feet, then travel wherever the wind takes it.

During your unforgettable voyage, you'll float above the treetops and below the clouds for about an hour, as the balloon travels between five and 10 miles. It's during this time you'll want to propose, as you take in the breathtaking scenery and enjoy this once-in-a-lifetime flight experience.

Upon landing, you and your girlfriend (along with the pilot and any other passengers) will celebrate with a champagne toast as the balloon is being rolled up. The whole experience takes about three hours. Keep in mind, most hot air balloon companies are located in rural areas, within a 90-minute drive from a major U.S. city. Balloon pilots usually operate from farms, parks, and fields with a lot of open space.

When making your reservation, for more money, you can arrange for you and your girlfriend (along with the pilot) to be the only passengers on your hot air balloon flight. All flights are subject to good weather conditions, so if you're planning to propose on a specific date, you might need a backup plan for popping the question in case the weather doesn't cooperate.

The United States Hot Air Balloon Team and 1-800-SKYRIDE.com also allow you to charter a hot air balloon ride virtually anywhere in America. If you and your significant other are a bit more adventurous, you can also coordinate sky diving and hang gliding rides through these companies.

When You Wish Upon a Star, Your Disney World Proposal Will Come True

Proposal Concept: Propose in the Magic Kingdom, in front of the castle, at The Disney World Resort, Disneyland, Disneyland Paris, or the Tokyo Disney Resort.

Approximate Scenario Cost: Varies.
Plus the cost of the engagement ring, if used.

Approximate Preparation Time: Several weeks.

Supplies/Equipment Needed: None.

Location: Orlando, Florida; Anaheim, California; Paris, France; or Tokyo, Japan.

Related Contact Information/Resources:

> Disney Reservations and Information
> 407-WDW-MAGIC
> *www.Disney.com*
>
> Disney's Fairy Tale Weddings
> 321-939-4610
> *www.disneyweddings.com*

For a multitude of reasons, a visit to any of the Disney theme parks can easily become a magical and memorable experience, especially if you and your girlfriend are young at heart and have fond memories of watching Disney movies or visiting the Disney theme parks as children. What could be more magical than allowing your girlfriend to get caught up in the fantasy of becoming a princess and being proposed to at the entrance to the castle in the Magic Kingdom, for example.

For couples enjoying a romantic getaway, honeymoon, or even their wedding reception, Walt Disney World in Orlando (or any of the other Disney theme parks) offers a multitude of things to see and do that will help you create a vacation experience you'll both fondly remember. A team of highly trained Disney Wedding Consultants can be reached by calling Disney's Fairy Tale Weddings at 321-939-4610 or by visiting *www.disneyweddings.com*. With a bit of help, you can plan the perfect way to pop the question—Disney style—while visiting the Walt Disney World Resort.

If you'd rather propose in privacy, you can arrange for a romantic dinner for two, for example, plus pay to have Mickey Mouse (or any of the Disney characters) participate in your proposal and assist you in popping the question. Contact the concierge at your Disney-owned hotel or resort for details.

For approximately $42,000, you can also arrange to have The Magic Kingdom at Disney World all to yourself for an after-hours engagement party. Contact the specialists at Disney's Fairy Tale Weddings to learn about all of the possible options for popping the question while vacationing at The Walt Disney World Resort in Orlando or any of the Disney theme parks.

Transform Your Proposal Into a Circus Act

Proposal Concept: Become part of The Big Apple Circus and pop the question under the circus big top with the help of the circus cast.

Approximate Scenario Cost: The price of two circus admission tickets (about $100 per couple).
Plus the cost of the engagement ring, if used.

Approximate Preparation Time: One to two weeks.

Supplies/Equipment Needed: None.

Location: The closest city where the Big Apple Circus tours.

Related Contact Information/Resources:

The Big Apple Circus Business Office
212-268-2500
www.BigAppleCircus.org

The Big Apple Circus is a world-famous, not-for-profit, one-ring circus that travels throughout America entertaining people of all ages. Performed under a traditional circus tent (measuring 47 feet high by 137 feet in diameter), circus performers from throughout the world allow spectators to enjoy the show from less than 50 feet from the ring. Each year, The Big Apple Circus visits New York City, Washington DC, Atlanta, Boston, and several other U.S. cities.

Featuring clowns, acrobats, trained animals, tightrope walkers, trapeze artists, juggling, and a host of other mesmerizing traditional (and not-so-traditional) circus acts, simply watching a performance of The Big Apple Circus is a fun and memorable experience in itself. If, however, you'd like to make your evening at the circus even more special by popping the question to your girlfriend—either during the show's intermission or immediately afterward—circus founder and artistic director Paul Binder extends a special invitation.

According to Binder:

> During The Big Apple Circus's 25-year history, a handful of couples have gotten engaged under our big top, with the help of our performers. During intermission or immediately after the show, we can invite you into the ring, where, with the help of our cast members, you can pop the question in front of the audience....Each time someone has proposed under our big top, it was a wonderful, powerful, and emotional experience for everyone. In each case, the woman being proposed to was totally surprised by the events that unfolded. The proposals were also featured in the local newspaper.

To coordinate your circus proposal, Binder suggests contacting The Big Apple Circus's main office in New York or the local production office in your city at least two weeks in advance. As long as your proposal idea doesn't disrupt the show or the performers' schedule, Binder enjoys helping couples get engaged in the most fun and memorable way possible.

For a more intimate or private engagement event, performers from The Big Apple Circus can be hired for private functions by contacting the "Circus To Go" coordinators at Wizard Productions (914-777-0900).

A view of the Big Apple Circus tent.

Propose on a Cruise Ship

Proposal Concept: Take a romantic high-seas cruise and propose at sunset, from the ship's deck or from another romantic location aboard the cruise ship.

Approximate Scenario Cost: $1,000 and up (per couple).
*Plus the cost of the engagement ring, if used.

Approximate Preparation Time: Several weeks.

Supplies/Equipment Needed: None.

Location: Most cruises leaving from the United States depart from Miami, however, there are cruises departing regularly from New York, Los Angeles, and other major U.S. ports. Popular cruise destinations include: Caribbean/Bahamas, Mexico, Panama Canal, Bermuda, Europe, Alaska, and Hawaii.

Related Contact Information/Resources:

Carnival Cruise Lines
888-CARNIVAL
www.carnivalcruiselines.com

Celebrity Cruise Lines
800-722-5941
www.celebrity.com

Disney Cruise Lines
800-951-3532
http://disneycruise.disney.go.com

Holland America Cruise Lines
877-724-5425
www.hollandamerica.com

Hotwire.com
(discount travel Website)
800-CRUISING
www.hotwire.com

Norwegian Cruise Lines
800-327-7030
www.ncl.com

Orbitz.com
(discount travel Website)
www.Orbitz.com

Priceline.com
(discount travel Website)
800-896-7552
www.priceline.com

Princess Cruise Lines
800-PRINCESS
www.princess.com

Royal Caribbean Cruise Lines
800-398-9819
www.RoyalCaribbean.com

Travelocity.com
(discount travel Website)
www.travelocity.com

Whether you're looking for a relaxing getaway or an action-packed vacation that's complete with exotic destinations and nonstop activities, experiencing a three-, five-, seven-, or 10-day cruise (or longer) can provide the backdrop to transform a romantic getaway into a memorable engagement celebration on the high seas.

Once aboard any of the popular cruise ships, no matter where it's headed, you'll have countless opportunities to pop the question in style. Some of the best places/times to propose on a cruise ship include:

➤ While strolling along the deck at sunset, alone with your significant other, taking in the spectacular view.

- ❧ During a romantic dinner in the ship's fanciest dining room.

- ❧ While sharing a toast or romantic time in the privacy of your cabin.

- ❧ During any of the ship's group activities.

- ❧ Before or after one of the ship's evening shows. (You can propose in front of the audience.)

- ❧ While experiencing any optional land excursion (at one of the ship's ports-of-call).

With the help of your ship's Cruise Director or any of the ship's crew, chances are you'll quickly come up with the absolute perfect way to propose. Each cruise ship line offers its own atmosphere, activities, and unique shipboard cruise experience. Some ships offer an abundance of activities for those who are more energetic and athletic, while others focus more on relaxation and romance. On some ships, experiencing extravagant, multicourse meals is a primary focus, while other ships offer more family-oriented entertainment.

If you decide you'd like to take your girlfriend on a cruise and pop the question during the voyage, it's important to work with a travel agent that specializes in booking cruises or to do your own research to ensure you select a cruise ship that offers the most of what you and your girlfriend will enjoy. Royal Caribbean, for example, is known for its spectacular stage shows, dining experiences, and activities (ranging from the onboard rock-climbing wall to the ice-skating rink). The Royal Caribbean ships are also equipped with world-class day spas, casinos, swimming pools, and a wide range of other indoor and outdoor activities.

After choosing your destination and ship, then booking your reservation, start thinking about how you'd like to propose during the cruise and what arrangements will need to be made. Many of the cruise ship lines will work with you in advance to plan the perfect proposal. Once onboard, you should definitely contact the ship's Cruise Director and discuss your plans in order to make additional special arrangements, such as having one of the ship's photographers on hand to capture the moment or having the ship's Captain propose a toast during or after dinner, once your girlfriend accepts your proposal.

Cruise ships provide an extremely romantic setting for getting engaged, plus, if you visit the various travel-related Websites, you're apt to find drastically discounted rates on many of the most popular cruise ships. The key to enjoying your cruise and making it as memorable as possible is proper planning, especially when it comes to how you'll spend your time at the various ports-of-call. Prebook your land-based excursions and pay careful attention to the daily schedule provided to passengers during each day of the cruise.

If you're traveling to Hawaii or the Caribbean, for example, when visiting one of the ports-of-call, you may choose to experience a submarine ride, go horseback riding, swim with dolphins, or explore ancient ruins. Any of these outings also offer excellent backdrops for popping the question, especially if you and your girlfriend share mutual interests that you can experience during your cruise.

Many of the cruise lines offer special "Romance Packages" for an additional fee. One package offered by Royal Caribbean (800-722-5443), for an additional $250 per couple includes:

- A "Welcome Aboard" bottle of Veuve Cliquot and canapés for two.

- Fresh-cut flowers in your cabin.

- Two waffle-woven robes.

- Breakfast for two delivered to your stateroom.

- Predinner canapés on two "formal" nights.

- After dinner sweets on two "formal" nights.

- A formal 8 x 10-inch portrait in a silver-plated frame.

It's always best to book your travel as far in advance as possible, especially if you're hoping to make special arrangements in order to propose. However, because of the abundance of cruise ships departing every week (from places like Miami, Florida), even if you decide to take a cruise last minute, you're apt to be able to book a reservation with relative ease. When shopping for the best deals, look for all-inclusive packages that include airfare, cruise accommodations, land-based transfers, and so on. The land-based excursions at the various ports-of-call typically cost extra and the rates quoted for the cruises do not include tips for your cabin attendant, waiter, and the like. While meals and snacks aboard the ship are included in the price of the cruise, drinks (alcoholic or nonalcoholic) typically cost extra.

If spending romantic quality time alone with your significant other at sea is important to you, you might consider chartering a crewed private yacht for an evening or weekend and taking a sail or cruise to a remote tropical location. The captain of the privately chartered boat will help you coordinate the details of your proposal aboard the yacht by helping you plan the perfect meal and choose a romantic spot to sail to, for example. After popping the question, you can enjoy scuba diving, snorkeling, fishing, or simply relaxing on deck and taking in the sun. An eight-hour sail aboard a crewed, 44-foot yacht, leaving from Ft. Lauderdale, Florida, for example, will cost about $900, plus extras, such as a licensed Captain and mate or cook (an additional $150 per day, per crew member).

For an unforgettable private sail aboard The Prelude, a 54-foot sailing vessel, that can take you for a sail around Manhattan Island for spectacular views of the Statue of Liberty and the New York City skyline, contact New York Boat Charter at 888-755-BOAT (*www.nyboatcharter.com*). For this type of private romantic cruise, plan on spending at least $250 per hour, plus the price of a multicourse meal aboard, docking fees, and taxes.

To find other yacht charter companies throughout the coastal areas of the United States, point your Web browser to CharterNet.com (*www.charternet.com/brokers/ index.html*) for a nationwide listing of yacht charter companies and brokers. When chartering a yacht or luxury sailing vessel, you must decide several things in advance, such as the type of boat you'd like to charter, where you'd like the cruise to begin and to go, how long you'd like the journey to last, and what special plans (such as romantic meals) are necessary to make your proposal unforgettable. Based on your budget, these are all things you should discuss in advance with the various charter companies.

Hire a Marching Band

Proposal Concept: Catch your girlfriend's attention by having a marching band perform as you prepare to pop the question.

Approximate Scenario Cost: Varies.
  Plus the cost of the engagement ring, if used.

Approximate Preparation Time: Several weeks.

Supplies/Equipment Needed: A high school or college marching band or drum line.

Location: Any.

Related Contact Information/Resources:

   Contact the music director at your local high school, college, or university.

What's the difference between half time at a high school or college football game and a marriage proposal? The answer can be very little if you recruit a marching band or drum line to help you score when proposing to your girlfriend.

You'll certainly get her attention when a marching band or drum line performs in the background as you march up to her, drop down to one knee, present her with an engagement ring, and propose. This can be done at a football game, during the marching band or drum line's rehearsal, or by coordinating a private performance exclusively for your girlfriend.

The easiest way to find a marching band or drum line to help make this type of proposal a reality is to contact the music director at your local high school, college, or university. To get the marching band or drum line to participate in this non-school-oriented activity may require that you make a financial donation to the school or its music department.

If you're not a big football fan, check out the movie *Drum Line* (20th Century Fox, *www.drumlinemovie.com*) on video or DVD to see just how exciting a marching band or drum line performance can be. This movie should give you a bunch of ideas about how you could score a touchdown by incorporating this type of exciting live musical performance into your marriage proposal.

Have a Custom Proposal Song Written and Recorded

Proposal Concept: Hire a professional singer, songwriter, and musician to write and record a song that's totally personalized for your girlfriend and that musically pops the question in a romantic way. You ultimately play a CD containing the song for your girlfriend as you present the engagement ring to her.

Approximate Scenario Cost: $1,000 to $1,500.
   *Plus the cost of the engagement ring.

Approximate Preparation Time: Two to four weeks.

Supplies/Equipment Needed: CD player to play the song for your girlfriend.

Location: Any.

Related Contact Information/Resources:

> Ferras
> E-mail: FerrasEmail@aol.com
> *www.FerrasMusic.com*
>
> Fronhofer Multimedia
> *www.fronhofer.com/gifts.htm*
>
> Pecora Creative Music
> *www.pecoracreativemusic.com/home*

Almost every couple has a favorite recording artist and a special song that's sentimental. You and your future spouse can kick off your engagement with a memorable and romantic song that is written and recorded specifically for you both.

Your girlfriend will be totally surprised when she inserts a CD she believes to be a collection of songs you compiled for her, but quickly discovers the CD contains a custom written and original song that ends with your musical proposal of marriage. Singer, songwriter, and pianist Ferras will write and record a custom song, based on information you provide about your girlfriend and your relationship together. The song will be recorded in a professional recording studio with full piano accompaniment, then sent directly to you on CD. Ferras will offer a preview of the song over the phone, so it can be further enhanced (if necessary) to meet the client's needs. Occasionally he can even be hired to perform the customized song live (along with other romantic music) at a reception, party, or other special event.

About his customized proposal song sevices, Ferras explains:

> For guys looking to pop the question to their girlfriend, I can write a song that musically conveys romantic thoughts and emotions someone may be uncomfortable or too shy to otherwise share in person. The song will be custom written and can incorporate information, sentiments, facts, and ideas that you provide. I'll write the lyrics, develop the music, and record the final song. When you're ready to propose, all you need to do is insert the CD in a player, have your girlfriend listen, and present the ring.

Two other companies that offer similar services are Pecora Creative Music and Fronhofer Multimedia. Pecora Creative Music offers all styles of custom love songs and music for any occasion, with personalized lyrics, professional instrumental background tapes, and/or as piano arrangements with guitar chords, by Jane Pecora. Through Fronhofer Multimedia, Heather Richards offers personalized songs custom written for any special occasion, or will even set your own poem or lyrics to music.

The beauty of having a custom proposal song written is that it allows the song's lyrics to musically reenact the time you first met, describe your overall relationship, communicate specific sentiments, and somehow incorporate your personalized marriage proposal. This song will be something you and your soon-to-be-wife will treasure for many years to come.

Hire a Professional Chef and Musicians for a Romantic Dinner at Home

Proposal Concept: Instead of going out for a formal dinner, bring the chef and live entertainment to your home for a romantic and intimate evening.

Approximate Scenario Cost: $500 to $2,000 (or more) depending on the chef, staff, and musicians you hire.

    *Plus the cost of the engagement ring, if used.

Approximate Preparation Time: Several weeks.

Supplies/Equipment Needed: Hire a professional chef, server, and musicians, plus create a romantic atmosphere in your home. This might include fancy table linens, candles, a fire in the fireplace, and so on.

Location: Your home or your girlfriend's home.

Related Contact Information/Resources:

    Private Chefs, Inc.
    310-278-4707
    www.privatechefsinc.com

    The Lawrence Group: A Culinary Agency
    202-588-7311
    www.culinaryagency.com

While you can create a romantic and memorable evening (perfect for popping the question) by taking your girlfriend to dinner at a fancy restaurant, you can create an even more intimate and memorable experience if you transform your dining room (or living room) into a five-star restaurant exclusively for you and her.

Transforming your home (or the home of your significant other) into the perfect romantic setting to propose might involve setting the dinner table using fancy dishes and silverware, lighting candles, and creating an extremely romantic mood. To make the evening even more special, however, you might want to hire a professional chef to come to your house and prepare a multicourse meal, plus hire a violinist, for example, to serenade you as you enjoy your fine meal and prepare to pop the question.

If you don't already own fine china and table linens, you might want to purchase or borrow settings for two to help create a romantic and formal dining experience in your home. You'll find adding some candles, dimming the lights, and lighting a fire in the fireplace can all contribute to the ambiance. Hiring one or two professional musicians to serenade you can be a wonderful touch, however, it's important to find the perfect professional chef to create a memorable meal you'll both enjoy.

To find a chef, start by contacting your favorite restaurants to see if the chef can be hired for one night to prepare a meal in your home. If there's a Bread & Circus, Whole Foods Market, or another high-end or gourmet supermarket in your area, you might be able to obtain a referral for a private chef from them. Another option is to contact a local culinary school or check the Yellow Pages for private chefs or caterers in your area. As you're deciding who to hire, consider the type of meal you would like to have prepared, then find someone who specializes in that type of food.

With a little research, you'll be able to find a professional chef that specializes in Italian, Chinese, Japanese,

America, vegetarian, or any other type of cooking. Once you've found the chef, work with him or her to plan a special menu, focusing on your girlfriend's favorite foods. The chef will do all of the necessary food shopping and handle all aspects of the meal preparation and clean up. For dessert, not only will you want something sweet, but make sure you have a bottle of wine or champagne chilled and ready to serve to toast your engagement.

Determine if the chef you hire will also act as the server. If not, you might also want to hire a professional server (accommodator) for the night, to create a true fine dining experience. Because you're going through the effort to create the perfect dining experience, be sure to enjoy the meal and dessert, then propose in whatever manner you feel is appropriate. Remember, you want to focus on creating a romantic situation that your girlfriend will appreciate and cherish for many years to come.

In the Southern California area, Private Chefs, Inc., is a service that hires out award-winning chefs for single day assignments or full-time employment. According to the company's Website (*www.privatechefsinc.com*):

> At Private Chefs, Inc., we provide the highest caliber of culinary service to a select clientele. A professional chef will become your personal chef for a day. After a brief consultation, your gourmet chef will create a menu specifically for you and your event, tailored around your culinary wishes. Your private chef will then create a schedule for the event and an estimate of purchases and personal time. Depending on the requirements of the event, your chef can arrange for any necessary services or bar staff.

The Lawrence Group, based in Washington, DC, is another well-established private chef placement agency.

Keep in mind, in the culinary world, a private chef is someone who has been trained at a recognized culinary school. A personal chef, however, may not have that formal training.

Korbel Champagne Cellars Shares Additional Proposal Ideas

When it comes to commemorating special occasions and holidays, or sharing a romantic moment with someone special, toasting that event and celebrating over a glass of champagne has become a tradition. Since 1882, Korbel (*www.Korbel.com*) has been sharing special moments with people. It is the highest selling premium champagne in the United States.

With the knowledge that popping the question often involves a romantic toast between the newly engaged couple (and possible bystanders), Korbel has set out to discover some of the most romantic and unique ways people choose to get engaged, then help some of the people who develop those ideas make them a reality, no matter how extravagant the ideas happen to be. In 2002, the first annual *Korbel Perfect Proposal Contest* was held, and the company received hundreds of fun, exciting, and unique marriage proposal ideas.

Each year, three contest winners not only get all of the help needed to make their dream proposal a reality, but Korbel picks up the tab and also provides a one carat diamond engagement ring to the winning couples. For one grand prize winner, Korbel also kicks in $10,000 to pay for the couple's engagement party, wedding reception, or honeymoon.

Three winning proposal scenarios from the 2002 contest are described here, plus Korbel's experts offer their strategies and describe the steps taken to make the winning proposal scenarios a reality and successfully execute the ideas. Today, the three couples described in the following sections are happily married, after getting engaged in very unique and memorable ways.

Broadway Proposal—New York, NY

When visiting New York City for the first time, many people enjoy experiencing the restaurants, traveling through Central Park, viewing the tourist attractions, and seeing a Broadway show. Ashley Yablon from Dallas, Texas, wanted to do all of this with his girlfriend, plus during their trip, pop the question.

Coming up with the idea to simply propose somewhere in New York City wasn't what allowed Ashley to be the grand prize winner of the Korbel Perfect Proposal Contest in 2002. He wanted his proposal to be star-studded and special. For as long as Ashley knew his girlfriend, Donna, she expressed dreams of visiting New York and being swept off her feet on Broadway.

Taking this as his queue, Ashley wanted to propose on the Broadway stage after serenading his girlfriend with a song that he performed live, in front of a sold-out audience. It was after a performance of Elton John's and Time Rice's *Aida*, that Ashley was given his big chance as a Korbel Perfect Proposal Contest winner. He excused himself from his seat just prior to the show ending, under the pretence of using the restroom. Instead, he was escorted backstage. After the show's finale, the cast invited Ashley on stage to sing to his girlfriend.

After his performance, Ashley invited Donna on stage. At this point, Donna still had no clue about what was about to happen. In front of everyone, Ashley dropped to one knee on stage and proposed. Donna quickly accepted and received a standing ovation from the *Aida* cast and audience. It was a trip to New York City she'll never forget.

Korbel's Expert Tips

To recreate a "Broadway" proposal, try contacting the public relations office at your favorite theater or from your favorite show in New York City. Locally, in your hometown, you could work with a local theater group and ask for permission to perform your proposal during intermission or after the show. Again, the public relations office is probably the best place to start.

Live proposals are great crowd-pleasers and many theatre groups are willing to help you make your dream proposal a reality. They can even help you by providing you with special center stage seating, getting group seats for family and friends, allowing you to stand in front of the live audience onstage during your proposal, involving the cast and crew, and including a *Playbill* or program insert. This type of proposal could also be recreated at a local movie theatre or outdoor performance venue. You just need a stage and the guts to get on it.

Ski Proposal—Steamboat Springs, CO

Brad Moline from Fort Collins, Colorado, along with his girlfriend, Courtney, are avid skiers and often enjoy ski trips to various ski resorts together. On one particular skiing adventure, Brad's plans involved a bit more than simply conquering the slopes. For all her life, Courtney's favorite ski area has been Steamboat Springs, Colorado. It was there that her grandfather (a former Steamboat ski instructor) taught her how to ski as a child. Thus, the ski resort held a lot of sentimental memories for Courtney. With the help of Korbel, it now holds one more special memory—as the place she became engaged.

During what Courtney thought was an ordinary trip down the slopes, Brad stopped midway down the run, seeming to enjoy the scenery. Of course, Courtney stopped as well. It was then that a parade of tuxedo-wearing ski instructors came skiing down the mountain in formation, carrying roses, champagne, and a 20 x 40-foot banner that read, "Will You Marry Me?" The parade ended directly in front of Brad and Courtney.

Dressed in his ski outfit, Brad dropped to one knee and proposed. He then helped Courtney remove her thick ski gloves in order to place the diamond engagement ring on her finger as the crowd comprised of ski instructors and fellow skiers cheered.

Korbel's Expert Tips

To create a unique proposal on the slopes at your favorite ski resort, try contacting the public relations or management office to determine whether you can work hand-in-hand with them to really make your proposal something special. (You could always propose at the top of your favorite run, but working with the PR team may allow you to enhance your proposal.) For example, many ski resorts host evening "torch parades" during high season, which you could try to be involved in. The ski resort may also allow you to place a special banner or sign on the mountain. Consider working with the staff to plan a creative visual display.

Aerial Proposal—Minneapolis, MN

Using the premise that he was taking his girlfriend, Denise, on a romantic weekend ski trip, Drew Mitchell from Minnetonka, Minnesota, boarded a small plane with her and a handful of other passengers. Little did Denise know, the jet was chartered by Korbel and the other passengers were helping to coordinate a special aerial marriage proposal.

A few minutes into the flight, Mitchell directed Denise to look outside the window, down onto the frozen lake below. It was then she spotted a giant message, written in 5-foot-by-8-foot letters, that read "Will you marry me?"

On the small plane, Mitchell dropped to one knee and proposed, while the other passengers, who were really Korbel employees, prepared some champagne for a toast after the plane returned to the airport, where family and friends were waiting to congratulate the newly engaged couple. Needless to say, Denise was extremely surprised.

Korbel's Expert Tips

Aerial proposals can be done from an airplane, hot-air balloon, helicopter, or even while parasailing. To recreate an aerial proposal, you first need to decide what your preferred method of transportation is. You can work with a local, small airport if you would like to propose from a plane, by chartering a private flight and a pilot. (Don't forget, you'll need a good story to fool your intended so she'll travel with you on the plane.)

Unless you are placing your proposal display on private property which you own, you may need to secure permits (such as if you are proposing at a park) from your local park district or city hall a few weeks in advance in order to place your display and do fly-overs. Your pilot will be able to educate you on how high you can fly and where you can fly, but you will also need to work with family and friends or an event design company to create your display. For Drew and Denise, the display was placed atop of the frozen Bryant Lake.

It is important to calculate how high you will be flying, in order to know how big your display should be. Take a practice run without your girlfriend to make sure you can see the special note. Also, have a rain day scheduled as a backup date. You message could be placed on snow, ice, or even on an open field or beach. For example, you could use hay bales, wooden letters, sand, lights, or people to spell out your proposal question. Be creative! For this type of proposal, the sky truly is the limit!

You Could Be Korbel's Next "Perfect Proposal Contest" Winner!

If you're thinking about popping the question and believe you've come up with a proposal scenario that's truly unique and romantic, consider participating in Korbel's annual Perfect Proposal Contest by visiting Korbel's Website at *www.Korbel.com*. To enter, submit a 250-word (or less) essay describing your perfect proposal. All entries are judged annually based on creativity, originality, and how romantic the theme is. Full details, along with additional information about past winners, can be found on the company's Website.

You Have Your Proposal Idea. Now What?

You've just read dozens of ideas about how you could pop the question in a fun, innovative, romantic, and memorable way. By combining elements of multiple ideas, you could easily create a marriage proposal scenario that you and your significant other will remember fondly for the rest of your lives.

Developing what you believe is the perfect marriage proposal idea is certainly a challenge, but it's just the first step toward successfully getting engaged. Once you know how you want to propose, you need to decide when to pop the question, choose the perfect engagement ring, and then start planning. The next chapter will help you organize, schedule, and successfully carry out your marriage proposal plan.

Chapter 4
Planning Your Proposal

nce you've come up with the perfect idea for how you want to propose, the next steps involve planning out every aspect of the proposal to ensure that it happens exactly as you've envisioned it, focusing carefully on all of the pertinent details. How much time you need to invest in planning your proposal will depend on how complex your proposal idea is to implement and the time it takes you to find and purchase the perfect engagement ring.

Depending on how extravagant your proposal idea is, you might seek out the help of a professional wedding planner, event planner, or travel agent to help you coordinate all of the details and make your plan a reality. Will You Marry Me? Proposal Planners (*www.2propose.com*, e-mail: vip@2promose.com), for example, is a nationally recognized provider of marriage proposal services. The company offers consulting and coordinating services to help its clients create and execute the most spectacular proposal scenario possible.

This chapter will help you plan your proposal so that, when the time comes to pop the question, you're able to create the romantic moment that you're hoping to achieve.

5 Steps for Planning the Perfect Proposal

By now, you've probably begun formalizing your plans regarding how you'd like to propose. As you do this, be sure to consider all of the options available to you in terms of creating the perfect marriage proposal scenario. The following five steps will help you to coordinate and implement your plans:

1. Once you've devised the perfect way to pop the question, take a few minutes to consider exactly what your girlfriend wants. Ask yourself what *she* would consider to be the perfect, most romantic, and memorable marriage proposal possible. Will your idea live up to her expectations?

2. Set the time frame in which you plan to propose. Will you propose on a specific date, in conjunction with a holiday or birthday, for example? Once you have a proposal date in mind, you also now have a deadline to meet in terms of making all of the necessary arrangements leading up to your proposal.

3. Aside from you and your girlfriend, consider who will be present when you propose. Will

you pop the question when you and your girlfriend are alone, or do you want friends, family, or others to witness this exciting event? Based on how you plan to pop the question, figure out all of the people who need to be involved in your proposal plans, including those who will be actively involved in making it happen as you've envisioned it.

4. Focus on the specifics regarding how you'll pop the question. Are you looking to capture the element of surprise? What needs to be done to ensure that you'll be able to make the necessary plans without your girlfriend discovering them too soon? Will your proposal be highly traditional and romantic, fun, or somewhat extravagant and outrageous? What do you plan to say as you pop the question?

5. Once you know how and when you'll propose and what type of scenario you'll create, proper planning is required to make sure every aspect of your scenario is well thought-out, coordinated, and rehearsed. Keep in mind, when the time comes to actually pop the question, you're going to be nervous (even if you're almost positive your proposal will be accepted). Being properly prepared will help ensure that nothing goes wrong, even if you're not thinking clearly, due to nervousness, when you actually propose.

Defining Your Proposal Plans

Take a few minutes to write out, in detail, how you plan to propose based on the idea(s) you've generated. Describe the scenario as you'd like it to unfold when the time comes for it to actually happen.

_____

_____

_____

_____

_____

_____

_____

_____

_____

_____

_____

_____

_____

Once you've created the perfect proposal scenario, selected the perfect location, and know when you plan to pop the question, think carefully about what you'd like to say when you actually propose. Consider this: You're down on one knee and you're looking directly into your girlfriend's loving eyes. You've set the stage for the perfect proposal. In your pocket is the engagement ring you're about to present. Now, what are you going to say and how are you going to say it?

Make a list of five or 10 important points you'd like to somehow work into what you plan to say as you pop the question.

Points To Make When Actually Proposing

1. _____
2. _____
3. _____
4. _____
5. _____
6. _____
7. _____
8. _____
9. _____
10. _____

Use this list as your outline for specifically what you plan to say as you pop the question. While you don't necessarily need or want to memorize a speech word-for-word, it's an excellent strategy to rehearse what you plan to say and exactly how you plan to say it. Obviously, you'll want to declare your love to your girlfriend. There are countless ways this can be done, however, so it's important to consider exactly what you want to say and what you think your significant other would like to hear. Keep in mind that, when you're actually proposing, you're probably going to be nervous, so by rehearsing, you'll be more apt to remember everything you'd like to say and do.

The Preproposal To-Do List

You've probably figured out that there are dozens of details that need to be attended to, in order to make your proposal happen the way you envision it. To help ensure that you don't forget anything, fill in the following information:

Today's Date:_____

Date/Time You Plan To Propose:_____

Days Remaining Until Your Proposal:_____

Taking into account your proposal scenario, what steps need to be done (and in what order) to implement your proposal on the date you've set? Consider everything that needs to be done, including finding and purchasing the engagement ring, making all reservations relating to the proposal, ordering items you plan to use to help you propose, etc. Don't forget to list all of the small details that need to be handled prior to your proposal, such as buying flowers and champagne.

To keep track of to-do items and schedule your time appropriately, consider using a day planner or scheduling software on your computer, or use the chart on the following page.

Prioritizing Your To-Do Task List

Once your preproposal to-do list is created, spend a few minutes prioritizing each item. You want to put your main focus on completing the most important and time-sensitive tasks first.

	Preproposal To-Do List		
Priority (1–4)	Task to Accomplish	Start Date	Completion Date

In the left column, labeled "Priority," place a 1 next to items that are the *most important* to complete or that are extremely time sensitive. Place a 2 next to items that are *important*, but not necessarily time critical. Place a 3 next to other items that need to be accomplished before you pop the question, but that can be completed after you've completed the more important or time-sensitive tasks. Finally, place a 4 next to the least important items that you'd like to get done, assuming you have time before your proposal deadline.

Contact Information

Keep track of all the people with whom you're in contact relating to your marriage proposal. Make sure you add everyone even remotely involved, such as the jeweler, photographer, and restaurant manager (where you plan to propose), to your contact list so that you have all of the necessary information in one place. You can keep track of this information on paper, in a day planner, or electronically using contact management software (such as Microsoft Outlook or Act!) or a Personal Digital Assistant (PDA).

For each contact, write down the following information:

Contact Information

Company:_____

Type of Business/Responsibility:_____

Contact Person:_____

Alternate Contact Person:_____

Address:_____

_____

Phone:_____

Fax:_____

E-mail: _____

Date of Initial Contact:_____

Follow Up Date(s):_____

Completion Dates:_____

Notes:_____

The Clock Is Ticking: Countdown to Your Engagement

Now that you've decided when you plan to pop the question, the clock is constantly ticking down to that all-important moment. Refer back to your to-do list often and make sure everything that's required is happening on schedule. One of the worst things you can do at this point is leave things until the last minute. The more time you spend handling all of the details relating to your proposal plans, the smoother things will be as you get closer to the actual date you plan to pop the question.

Some things, such as finding and purchasing the perfect engagement ring, choosing where you want to propose, and deciding how you'll actually pop the question are things that shouldn't be rushed. If you're working under a tight deadline (because you've decided to propose on a specific date that's approaching quickly), make sure you'll be able to accomplish everything that's necessary to successfully execute your proposal plans in the time available to you. Planning an exotic trip or implementing many of the proposal ideas described in Chapter 3, for example, will require at least several weeks to properly plan, so schedule your time accordingly.

Finally, if there's a lot that needs to be accomplished before you actually pop the question, consider recruiting one or more close friends or family members to help you coordinate all of your plans. Because you should always be thinking about what your girlfriend will think about your plans and how she'll react when you actually propose, you might also seek out the advice or guidance of her closest friends or family members, providing they'll be able to keep your secret until you actually pop the question.

Yes, there's a lot for you to do before you actually propose to your significant other, however, this should be a fun and exciting time in your life. Don't allow the pressure of finding the "perfect" engagement ring or coming up with the very best way to propose get in the way of you enjoying this exiting and memorable time of your life. Now that you've chosen the person you want to marry, your life is about to change in a very positive way.

With all of the time and effort you'll put into creating the most incredible marriage proposal scenario possible, think how wonderful you and your girlfriend will feel when the moment comes for you to present the engagement ring to her and you actually ask for her hand in marriage. The look you see in her eyes, whether the proposal is a surprise or not, will be priceless—and something you'll both remember for the rest of your lives.

Chapter 5

The Answer Might Not Be "Yes"

While it's important to think positive and believe your girlfriend will accept your marriage proposal, no matter how much you love her and how serious you are about dedicating the rest of your life to making her happy as her husband, there's always a chance that your proposal *won't* be accepted.

This chapter is all about what happens if, after popping the question, your proposal is rejected. Obviously, this isn't something you want to happen, but on the off chance it does, you'll want to be prepared.

Reasons She Might Reject Your Proposal

Even if you know in your heart that your girlfriend loves you, there are many reasons why your marriage proposal might be rejected, including:

- The timing is bad. You and your girlfriend are at different points in your lives. For whatever reasons, she's not ready to get married right now.

- She doesn't feel the same way about you as you feel about her; she doesn't believe you're her true soul mate.

- There are differences between you and her that she believes can't be worked out. Compromises can't or won't be made.

- She's looking for someone with better financial stability or who is more responsible.

- Her parents don't approve of you and she's not willing to alienate her family.

- You don't share the same religious beliefs and her beliefs are keeping her from marrying outside of her religion.

- She doesn't believe you will be faithful.

- Your girlfriend doesn't believe she knows you well enough or it's too soon in the relationship for her to consider marriage.

- She is career-oriented and believes that getting married now (or in the next few months) would somehow interfere with her professional life.

-❀ She's been seeing someone else behind your back.

-❀ Your girlfriend didn't like the way you proposed to her.

-❀ Your girlfriend wants to someday raise a family, but she doesn't believe you will be a good father to her children. Perhaps you have very different family-oriented goals.

-❀ She's afraid.

There's Probably Still Hope for the Relationship

As you can see, some of the reasons why your proposal might be rejected are fixable and, with work, could be rectified. Perhaps what is needed is a greater level of trust and understanding between you and your girlfriend. For example, due to any number of reasons, your girlfriend may love you and want to marry you, but believes the timing just isn't right. This could, however, mean that in a few months or maybe a few years, the situation will change and she'll be more open to the idea and ready for marriage.

When two people are truly in love, making the decision to get married will probably be simple for both of you, despite whatever challenges you will have to face as a couple. You'll both be willing to accept one another for who you are, make compromises when necessary, and work together to confront life's many obstacles.

Love, however, can be a strange emotion. Even if you're head-over-heals in love with someone and willing to do virtually anything for them, it doesn't automatically mean that the person you're in love with feels the same way about you. Thus, when you decide to pop the question, there's always a chance that for any number of reasons, your proposal will be rejected.

Accepting a proposal is probably one of the most important decisions someone will have to make in their lifetime. It's a decision that shouldn't be made lightly. Just as you have had to evaluate a wide range of things about your girlfriend before popping the question, she needs to do the same in regard to you, before accepting your proposal.

So, what happens if your girlfriend—the person you're truly, madly, and deeply in love with—decides she doesn't want to marry you after you pop the question? Well, unfortunately, it'll probably be a tremendous blow to your ego and will most likely be an extremely upsetting occasion for you. You might also feel embarrassed, betrayed, mislead, confused, angry, and/or sad. Feeling any or all of these emotions is normal for someone in this situation.

Depending on why your proposal was rejected, there's probably a good chance you'll be able to change her mind and win her heart, if that's what you determine would be the best course of action at this point.

What To Do If You Are Rejected

Before doing anything rash, carefully evaluate the situation and determine exactly why your proposal was rejected. What emotions and thoughts drove your girlfriend to make the decision she did? Did your girlfriend reject the idea of getting married right now, or did she reject the idea of you *ever* becoming her husband? Put yourself in your girlfriend's shoes and try to understand her rationale for not accepting your proposal. Next, determine if and when you might be able to change her mind in the near future and what would be required to make this happen.

For example, if you're both in school, she might want to hold off on getting married until after you've both graduated and have jobs. This being the case, you might determine that in the foreseeable future (once you've both graduated), she will accept your proposal. The timing just isn't right for her now. Perhaps she's simply afraid. Fear can be a powerful emotion and keep her from following her heart. What can you do to understand and help alleviate her fears?

By honestly evaluating the situation if you are rejected, you should pretty easily be able to determine if there's any future long-term potential for your relationship. Based on why your proposal was rejected, you might decide to keep things status quo in your relationship right now and see how you progress over the next few months (or years, depending on the situation). You may, however, figure out that the person you thought would make the perfect spouse really isn't your ideal match after all.

If you determine that the reason for the rejection is one that can't be fixed and no compromises can be made, look carefully at the potential future of the relationship (or lack thereof). Decide if you should break off the relationship and ultimately go your separate ways. Of course, this is an extremely difficult decision to make. However, if after having an open and honest conversation with your girlfriend, you determine that there's no hope of you two ever getting married, you'll probably want to move on with your lives. Whether or not you choose to remain friends is, of course, up to you. Whatever happens at this point, you can expect the next few days, weeks, or perhaps months to be difficult from an emotional standpoint.

Could a Rejection Be a Blessing in Disguise?

If your proposal gets rejected, look carefully at the big picture. You're better off discovering now that you and your girlfriend really aren't meant for each other. After all, things would be a lot tougher emotionally and financially if you were to get engaged, then break off the engagement a few weeks or months down the road.

Things would be even worse for you both if you ended up getting married, but quickly discover you weren't meant for each other. Far too many divorces happen because the people involved in the relationship weren't mature and responsible enough to confront their feelings and deal with the necessary issues *prior* to getting engaged and, ultimately, married. If your initial marriage proposal gets rejected, think carefully about whether you're making well-thought-out and mature decisions about your future.

Can You Salvage the Relationship?

If, after evaluating your girlfriend's rejection to your proposal, you believe there's a way to salvage the relationship, or even if you're not willing to give up just yet, here are a few steps you can take to possibly change her mind:

- Have a private, heart-to-heart talk with your girlfriend. Be open and totally honest with each other. Discuss all of the reasons why your proposal was rejected and determine exactly what you'd each need to do in order to remedy the situation and change her mind. Next, think about whether you're each willing to accept the responsibility required to make the necessary modifications to your relationship so that she'll be more comfortable accepting your proposal in the near future. Chances are, you'll both need to make some concessions to accommodate the other person's needs and desires. Are you willing to make them and live with the consequences?

-❧ Seek out the advice of family and close friends. It's possible you're too close to the situation and "blinded by love," which is keeping you from seeing the whole picture accurately. Look to the people close to you for advice and guidance. These people can also be a powerful support system if you determine the relationship is over.

-❧ Consult with your spiritual or religious leader—a priest, rabbi, minister, etc. These people are usually understanding and easy to talk to. They can offer you an unbiased perspective as well as relationship counseling.

-❧ Even though you're not yet married, consider meeting with a marriage counselor or participating in couple's therapy to work out your issues. Determine if there is still future potential for a positive and healthy relationship together. A therapist can also help you move on and deal with your emotions if you determine the relationship is truly over.

Obviously, if you've made the decision to propose, you hopefully have a pretty good inclination that your girlfriend's response will be yes. Just in case you're surprised by a rejection, however, don't immediately say or do anything rash that could jeopardize your future relationship. Keep your emotions in check until you determine exactly why your proposal was rejected, then act accordingly.

If you're honestly not sure how your girlfriend will respond to your proposal, but you know she's the person you want to marry, consider choosing a more private proposal scenario when it comes to popping the question. Instead of proposing in public, opt for a more intimate and private setting. This will help you avoid any embarrassment if your proposal gets rejected. You can obtain ideas for more private scenarios for popping the question from Chapters 2 and 3.

Chapter 6
Your Life After Getting Engaged

Once you've popped the question to your girlfriend and she accepts, you're officially engaged to be married and your girlfriend is now your fiancée! From the moment you become engaged to be married, life as you know it will change forever. In addition, events in your life will start happening extremely fast, so hold on and get ready for an exciting roller coaster ride. This chapter is all about what you can expect after you're engaged. It talks about some of the major events that will happen in your life leading up to the wedding.

Will You Marry Me? Popping the Question with Romance and Style is not a wedding planning guide nor was it written to take the place of a professional wedding planner. There are literally hundreds of books that will help you, your girlfriend, your parents, and your soon-to-be in-laws plan your wedding and honeymoon.

Announcing Your Engagement

One of the first things you'll want to do after getting engaged is announce it to the world—your family, friends, coworkers, etc. Once you start telling a few people, you'll be surprised how quickly news travels. Expect people to start coming up to you and calling with their congratulations, even if you didn't tell those people directly. Oh, and you can expect to receive engagement gifts as well.

It's best for the people who are close to you to hear about your engagement directly from you and your girlfriend. Thus, you should both make a list of the people in your lives who are most important to you, then make a point to call or speak with those people directly to tell them your exciting news. Depending on your personal situation, your parents and your soon-to-be in-laws, as well as your siblings and other close relatives, should be at the top of your lists, as should your closest friends.

Announcing your engagement is something you and your fiancée should do together (in person, whenever possible), at least when it comes to family and close friends. After all, she'll probably want to proudly show off her engagement ring (and brag about the guy who gave it to her). Be prepared to tell the story about how you popped the question over and over again.

Once you start telling people about your engagement, you're almost always going to be asked three questions:

1. When is the wedding?
2. Where will the wedding be held?
3. Where are you going on your honeymoon?

Don't worry. It's very common for newly engaged couples not to have answers to these questions right away. You can respond by saying something like, "We just got engaged. We're still exploring our options." After all, an engagement can last anywhere from a few weeks to two years or more, depending upon your personal situations. The average length of an engagement in America is 16 months.

Once you've announced your engagement to the people who are important to you both, consider sending out more formal engagement announcement cards. Any local print shop will allow you to order custom-printed cards announcing your engagement. These cards can be used simply to announce that you're engaged, or you can inform people when you'll actually be getting married and request that they save the date. Send the cards to your family, friends, coworkers, members of your church/ temple (or religious organization), and anyone else who is important to you and your betrothed. You might want to review the list of people to whom you'd typically send a holiday card, in order to ensure that you don't forget anyone. Be sure to keep your list handy; you'll want to revisit it when you start deciding who will be invited to the wedding.

While you can use your own creativity and wording, the following pages contain some sample wording for engagement announcement cards.

Save the Date

*John Doe and Jane Smith
are engaged!*

*The wedding celebration will be held on
Saturday, the seventeenth of July
Two thousand and four.*

Invitation to follow.

Sample engagement announcement card
(if you know the wedding date).

We're Tying the Knot

John Doe and Jane Smith

*The wedding celebration will be held on
Saturday, July 17, 2004
New York City*

Please save the date—invitation to follow.

Sample engagement announcement card
(if you know the wedding date).

On Saturday, June 7, 2003,

John Doe and Jane Smith
became engaged to be married.

Wedding ceremony and celebration details to follow.

Sample engagement announcement card
(if you do not yet know the wedding date).

John Doe
And
Jane Smith

[Insert photograph of
you and your girlfriend]

We're happy to announce our engagement!

Sample engagement announcement card
(if you do not yet know the wedding date).

Mr. and Mrs. Anna Smith are proud to announce
the engagement of their daughter,
Miss Jane Smith, to Mr. John Doe,
son of Mr. and Mrs. Simon Doe.

Jane and John are planning a summer 2004 wedding.

Sample engagement announcement card
(if you do not yet know the wedding date).

In addition to calling close relatives and friends, as well as sending out engagement announcement cards, you and your fiancée should consider submitting an announcement to your local newspaper(s). Virtually all newspapers publish engagement announcements. Contact the newspaper(s) in your hometown and your fiancée's hometown. You might also consider contacting the newspapers where each of your parents live, as well as where you each grew up.

Typically, to submit an engagement announcement to a newspaper, you'll need to contact the newspaper directly (call the newspaper's main phone number) and request an engagement announcement form, which must be filled out and submitted to the appropriate editor. When submitting information about your engagement to any newspaper, type (rather than hand write) the information to help ensure accuracy. Also, determine if there's a fee to have your announcement published. Make sure you supply the correct spelling of each person's name, as well as accurate background information. You'll also want to provide the date you'd like the announcement to be published.

If you plan to submit an engagement photo to the newspaper with your announcement, make sure your names are clearly printed on the back of the photo. Chances are, your photo will not be returned, so make a copy to send to the newspaper. Finally, make sure your contact information (name, phone number, address, e-mail address, etc.) is clearly printed on the form, in case someone at the newspaper has any questions.

Take a look at a handful of engagement announcements published in your local newspaper to determine exactly what you'd like to say. Most engagement announcements in newspapers contain the following information:

- ✖ Full names of the bride and groom (no nicknames).
- ✖ Full names of the bride's and groom's parents.
- ✖ The planned wedding date (at least the month and year).
- ✖ The city and state where the wedding will be held.
- ✖ One line of background information about the bridge and groom, such as education or career-related details.

Many newspapers will either publish an engagement *or* a wedding announcement with a photo, so decide which is more important, after contacting the newspaper(s) to obtain their engagement announcement guidelines and submission form. You might consider waiting until six months prior to the wedding to have your engagement announcement published. This should allow ample time to plan the details of the wedding, such as the location and date.

It's Party Time!

If you're following "tradition" (and this term is being used lightly here), between the time you get engaged and the actual wedding, there will be a considerable amount of celebrating. You and your fiancée (or your parents or future in-laws) might decide to host an engagement party. This is a social gathering that can be very formal or as casual as a backyard barbecue. An engagement party is typically attended by the soon-to-be bride and groom, along with family, friends, coworkers, and anyone else you'd like to invite.

As you get closer to the wedding date, the soon-to-be groom may be invited by his best man to a bachelor party, while the bride gets whisked away by her bridesmaids for a bachelorette party. These tend generally to be "guys only" or "girls only" events.

Let the Planning Begin

Almost immediately after you get engaged, you will need to start the process of planning your wedding. Depending on the type of wedding you envision and the number of guests you plan to invite, this can become a tremendously time-consuming endeavor that will require you both to make literally hundreds of decisions. At the very least, you'll want to get your hands on at least one or two books about wedding planning, in order to help you take an organized approach to this process and keep costs under control. (An average wedding in America costs more than $20,000.) New Page Books (800-227-3371, *www.newpagebooks.com*) offers a number of wedding planning books covering everything from vows and toasts to budgeting and catering. You might also consider hiring a professional wedding planner to work with you to create your ultimate dream wedding.

As the wedding planning begins, everyone will have ideas about the date, location, theme, what food should be served, the music to be played, what the wedding party should wear, etc. Even if your parents or your in-laws are paying for the wedding and handling many of the details, it's extremely important that you and your fiancée remain the final decision-makers. After all, this is your wedding and it's important that you're actually able to experience the wedding you both envision.

One of the first decisions you'll need to make will involve the date for the wedding. Start off by choosing a month and year. This will give you a time frame in which you can plan the ceremony and celebration.

At the same time you're putting the wedding plans together, you'll also need to plan your honeymoon. About 99 percent of newly married couples go on a honeymoon and wind up spending, on average, about $4,000 for the trip. The average length of a honeymoon is nine days. Of course, this can vary based on your budget and interests.

Your honeymoon will be your first trip together as a married couple, so you want the trip to be extremely romantic and memorable. Spend some time deciding what type of honeymoon you'd both enjoy, then consult with a few travel agents that specialize in honeymoons to fine tune your ideas and narrow down the vast possibilities. You can also visit *www.HoneymoonLocation.com* or *www.VacationIdea.com* for ideas and trip-planning advice. If you're on a budget, take full advantage of online travel sites to save money. For example, at *www. Hotwire.com*, there is a special "Deals & Destinations" section that offers romantic getaway and honeymoon ideas that are discounted.

Honeymoon destination possibilities are limitless. Use this opportunity to visit somewhere exotic that you've always dreamed about. If you're planning to travel during a peak honeymoon season, such as June or July, it's best to make your travel reservations as far in advance as possible.

Some popular honeymoon destinations and ideas include:

- Taking a trip to somewhere tropical, such as Hawaii or the Caribbean, and staying at a beachfront resort.

- Going on a European sight-seeing adventure—London, Paris, Amsterdam, Italy, etc.

- Taking a cruise.

- Going to a romantic destination that's sentimental to you both.

- Traveling somewhere to enjoy some type of activity together, such as skiing, mountain climbing, camping, etc.

Congratulations on Your Engagement!

Well, you did it! You found the person of your dreams, are ready to pop the question, and are about to become engaged to be married! This is truly an exciting time in your life, so take the time to enjoy it. From this point on, you are a couple—a team—and must begin making decisions together, supporting each other, and working in unison to accomplish your mutual goals and dreams. Your two independent lives are coming together into one. Sure, there'll be plenty of adjustments required, but as you embark on your lives together as an engaged couple and ultimately as happily married partners, maintain an open, honest, and supportive line of communication. Never be afraid to remind each other how in love you are. Use the wedding planning process as practice for facing challenges and making important decisions together.

Hopefully, your proposal scenario will happen exactly the way you envision it. With proper planning and effort, your wedding day should be a similar success! If you propose in a fun, unique, and memorable way, and you'd like to share your experiences and ideas with others (possibly in future editions of this book), please e-mail the author, Jason R. Rich, at jr7777@aol.com, or visit his Website at *www.JasonRich.com*. We'd love to hear about how you incorporated the ideas from this book into your proposal.

Again, congratulations on your engagement. May your lives together as a couple be filled with love, happiness, health, and success!

Quick Reference Guide

Banners (Custom Made for Proposals)

Kinko's—*www.kinkos.com*, 800-2-KINKOS

Billboards

Ads On Wheels—*www.adsonwheels.com*,
800-237-6694

Electronic Marketing Company—
www.emc-outofhome.com, 610-353-9300

Outdoor Mobile Media—
www.outdoormobilemedia.com, 800-925-8772

Butterflies

The Butterfly Collection—*www.Bufferflycelebration.com*,
800-548-3284

Butterfly & Nature Gift Store—*www.butterfly-gifts.
com/livebutterflyreleases.html*, 888-395-7324

Amazing Butterflies—*www.amazingbutterflies.com/
basket.htm*, 800-808-6276

Castles

Pousadas de Portugal—*www.pousadas.pt*,
  Phone: +351 218 442 001, Fax: +351 218 442 085,
  E-mail: guest@pousadas.pt

Portuguese National Tourist Office—
  www.portugal.org, 800-PORTUGAL

Chefs

Private Chefs, Inc.—*www.privatechefsinc.com*,
  310-278-4707

The Lawrence Group: A Culinary Agency—
  www.culinaryagency.com, 202-588-7311

Chocolate

Godiva—*www.godiva.com*, 800-9-GODIVA

Circus

The Big Apple Circus (Business Office)—
  www.BigAppleCircus.org, 212-268-2500

Cookies (Specialized)

Cookies By Design—*www.CookiesByDesign.com*,
  800-945-2665

Costumes

Blacksmith Armor Sculptor—*www.thakblacksmith.com/
  html/rentals.html*, 519-669-0721

Costume World—*www.costumeworld.com/xmas.html*,
  800-423-7496

Planet Santa (Pierre's Costumes)—
  http://store.planetsanta.com or *www.costumers.com*,
  215-925-7121

Credit Card Offers

Bank Rates—*www.bankrate.com*
Card Locator—*www.cardlocator.com*
The Credit Card Catalog—
www.creditcardcatalog.com
The Credit Card Directory—
www.cardoffers.com
Credit Cards Plus—*www.credit-cards-plus.com*
CreditLand—*www.credit-land.com*

Credit Reports

Equifax—*https://www.econsumer.equifax.com/webapp/
ConsumerProducts/index.jsp*, 800-685-1111
P.O. Box 740241
Atlanta, GA 30374-0241
Experian (TRW)—*www.experian.com*,
888-EXPERIAN
P.O. Box 2002
Allen, TX 75013
Trans Union—*www.transunion.com*,
900-916-8800
P.O. Box 1000
Chester, PA 19022

Crossword Puzzles (Custom Made)

Crossword Weaver (software)—
www.crosswordweaver.com, 800-229-3939
1st Spot Crossword Puzzle Games—
http://1st-spot.net/topic_crosswords.html
CustomPuzzles.com—*www.custompuzzles.com*
Web Games To Go—*www.webgamestogo.com*

Barbara Johnson—812-332-3638,
E-mail: iambabs@aol.com
Master Puzzlers—*www.masterpuzzles.com,*
E-mail: TP@MasterPuzzles.com

Cruises

Carnival Cruise Lines—*www.carnivalcruiselines.com,*
888-CARNIVAL
Celebrity Cruise Lines—*www.celebrity.com,*
800-722-5941
Disney Cruise Lines—*http://disneycruise.disney.go.com,*
800-951-3532
Holland America Cruise Lines—
www.hollandamerica.com, 877-724-5425
Hotwire.com—*www.hotwire.com,* 800-CRUISING
New York Boat Charter—*www.nyboatcharter.com,*
888-755-BOAT
Norwegian Cruise Lines—*www.ncl.com,*
800-327-7030
Orbitz.com—*www.Orbitz.com*
Priceline.com—*www.priceline.com,* 800-896-7552
Princess Cruise Lines—*www.princess.com,*
800-PRINCESS
Royal Caribbean Cruise Lines—
www.RoyalCaribbean.com, 800-398-9819
Travelocity.com—*www.travelocity.com*

Diamonds and Engagement Rings

A Diamond is Forever—*www.adiamondisforever.com*
American Gem Society (AGS)—*www.ags.org,*
800-341-6214

Blue Nile, Inc—*www.bluenile.com*, 888-565-7610

Diamonds.com—*www.Diamonds.com*,
   877-956-9600

E-Wedding bands—*www.e-weddingbands.com*

Gemological Institute of America (GIA)—
   www.gia.org, 800-421-7250

Harry Winston—*www.harry-winston.com*
   718 Fifth Avenue
   New York, NY 10019
   212-245-2000

Jewelers of America (JA)—*www.jewelers.org*,
   800-223-0673

Moonstone Jewelry—*www.moonstone-jewelry.com*

PlatinumJewels.com—*www.platinumjewels.com*

TeNo—*www.TeNoUSA.com*

Titanium Era—*www.titaniumera.com*

Titanium Rings Studio—*www.tirings.com*

Disney

Disney Reservations and Information—
   www.Disney.com, 407-WDW-MAGIC

Disney's Fairy Tale Weddings—
   www.DisneyWeddings.com, 321-939-4610

Eiffel Tower

Main Website—*www.tour-eiffel.fr/teiffel/uk/*

Altitude 95 Restaurant—
   Phone: 33 (0)1 45 55 20 04

Le Jules Verne Restaurant—
   Phone: 33 (0)1 45 55 61 44

Fortune Cookies (with Special Proposal Mesage)

Fortune Cookie Supply Company—
www.fortunecookiesupply.com, 818-905-8180

Victory Store—*http://store.yahoo.com/victorystore00/
ilforcook.html*

Horse-Drawn Carriages

Boston Hansom Cabs—*www.bostonhansomcabs.com*,
781-391-3079

Directories—*www.angelfire.com/biz/
DieGelbeRoseCarriage/worldwide.html*,
www.bridalday.com/Transportation/more2.php3, or
*www.allweddingcompanies.com/Weddings/
Transportation/Carriages/*

Elegant Touch Carriage Company—
www.eleganttouchcarriage.com, 781-767-5819 or
800-497-4350

Hot Air Ballons

Soaring Adventures of America—
www.800soaring.com, 800-762-7464

The United States Hot Air Balloon Team—
www.ushotairballoon.com, 800-76-FLY-US

1-800-SKY-RIDE.com—*www.1800skyride.com*,
800-759-7433

Jewelry Insurance

Chubb Insurance Solutions—*www.chubbsolutions.com*,
877-972-8282 or 888-862-4822

Jewelers Mutual Insurance Company—
www.jewelersmutual.com, 800-558-6411

Korbel Perfect Proposal Contest

Korbel—*www.korbel.com*

Magic Tricks

Tannen's Magic—*www.tannens.com*, 212-929-4500
Airport Magic Shop—*www.AirportMagicShop.com*,
215-492-5171
MagicTricks.com—*www.MagicTricks.com*

Movie Theater Preshow Production Companies

National Cinema Network—*www.ncninc.com*,
800-SCREEN-1
Screenvision—*www.screenvision.com*,
212-497-0400

Music (Custom Written for Proposals)

Ferras—*www.FerrasMusic.com*,
E-mail: FerrasMusic@aol.com
Fronhofer Multimedia—
www.fronhofer.com/gifts.htm
Pecora Creative Music—
www.pecoracreativemusic.com/home

Newspapers

Directory—*www.newspaperlinks.com/home.cfm*.

Photo and Scrapbook Resources

Exposures—*www.exposuresonline.com*, 800-222-4947
Brookstone—*www.Brookstone.com*, 866-576-7337
Sharper Image—*www.SharperImage.com*, 800-344-4444

Planners

Will You Marry Me? Proposal Planners—
www.2propose.com, E-mail: vip@2promose.com

Poetry

America Online's Create A Love Poem (AOL Keyword:
Valentine Love Poetry)—
http://aolsvc.virtualpoetry.aol.com//feature/valentines
ILovePoetry.com—*www.ilovepoetry.com*

Puzzles (Custom Made)

Custom Puzzle Craft—*www.custompuzzlecraft.com,*
619-865-7774
MGC Custom Made Puzzles—*www.mgcpuzzles.com,*
888-604-7654

Radio Shows

American Top 40 with Casey Kasem—818-295-5800
Radio Express
1415 West Magnolia Blvd.
Burbank, California 91506

Hollywood Hamilton's Weekend Top 30—
www.weekendtop30.com, 866-HHT-TOP30
1158 26th Street, Box 440
Santa Monica, CA 90403-4698

Open House Party with John Garabedian
800-669-1010
www.openhouseparty.com

Rick Dees The Weekly Top 40—*www.rick.com,*
818-845-1027
KIIS-FM
3400 Riverside Drive, Suite 800
Burbank, CA 91505

Same-Sex Marriage

GLAD (Gay and Lesbian Advocate Defenders)— *www.glad.org*

Pride Bride—*www.pridebride.com*

Screen Saver Software

Screen Paver—*www.screenpaver.com*

ScreenTime Media—*www.screentime.com*

Screen Saver Maker—*www.screen-saver-maker.com*

Skywriting and Skytyping

Skytypers—*www.SkyTypers.com*, (East Coast) 718-507-5220, (West Coast) 562-598-8577, or (South East) 954-791-7936

Tom King Aerial Enterprises—800-995-KING

Directory—*www.pilotshack.com/AerialAdvertising.html*

Sporting Events

Fenway Park (Boston, MA)—877-RED-SOX9 or 617-375-0900

Yankee Stadium (New York, NY)— *http://newyork.yankees.mlb.com*, 718-579-4464

Stars (to Name a Star)

International Star Registry—*www.starregistry.com*, 800-282-3333

Star Foundation—*www.BuyAStar.net*, 888-877-STAR

Tatoos (Temporary)

Body Talk Temporary Word Tattoos—*http://romanceher.com/wordtatoos.htm*, 866-Send-A-Gift

Flax Art & Design—*www.flaxart.com*, 888-352-9278

Hearts Desire Gift Baskets (Body Talk Tattoo Set)—
http://heartsdesiregiftbaskets.safeshopper.com,
866-243-4249

Teddy Bears

Build-A-Bear Workshop—*www.buildabear.com*,
877-789-BEAR

Vermont Teddy Bear Company—
www.vermontteddybear.com, 800-829-BEAR

Television Networks

NBC (New York)—212-664-444

ABC (New York)—212-456-7777

CBS (New York)—212-975-4321

Index

About the Author

Jason R. Rich (*www.JasonRich.com*) is the author of more than 25 books on a wide range of topics. His recently published books include: *Brain Storm: Tap Into Your Creativity to Generate Awesome Ideas and Remarkable Results* (The Career Press), *Make Your Paycheck Last* (The Career Press), and a series of travel guides targeted to families. In late 2004, his book *The Bachelor's Guide to Life* will be published by New Page Books. He's also an accomplished newspaper and magazine columnist, and provides marketing, PR, and consulting services to numerous businesses. He lives just outside of Boston.